Toads for Supper

To be engaged to three girls simultaneously,
accused by one of being the father of her
child, rusticated by the University authorities—are severe setbacks in the career of
an undergraduate.

How Amadi got himself into this situation, and his efforts to extricate himself
from it, is the subject of this first novel. The
author's understanding, sympathy and in-
sight into the undergraduate life in Nigeria
today make this much more than the farce
that Amadi's predicament implies. Mixed
with the robust high spirits there is poetry
as well as tragedy, and an underlying
genuineness that makes this light-hearted
description of life in Nigeria both memor-
able and haunting.

African writers in the Fontana Modern Novels series

Toads for Supper

Vincent Chukwuemeka Ike

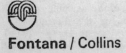

Fontana / Collins

First published by Harvill Press Ltd., May 1965
First issued in Fontana Books August 1965
Twelfth Impression July 1979

Made and printed in Great Britain by
Hunt Barnard Printing Ltd, Aylesbury, Bucks.

This book is a work of fiction. The
characters are imaginary, and any
resemblance to actual persons is
accidental

An explanation of the Nigerian expressions
used in the text is given by the author at
the end of the book

For 'Bimpe

I

' *Akwasa!* '

Amadi turned towards the object of attraction—a shapely girl, approaching them from Lugard Hall.

' She certainly belongs! ' declared Chima.

' Well, well! '

Chima turned to look at Amadi. ' You sound as if you knew her.'

The girl smiled at Amadi as she walked past. He replied with a smile that spread across his whole face and took an uncertain step towards her, checking himself when he saw she did not intend to stop. He and Chima followed her with their eyes till she disappeared into the Porter's Lodge of Macaulay Hall.

' Bo, dat one catch, O! '

' Well, I am flattered. It means mine are not the only eyes that can spot a ripe cob in a maize farm.'

' Come on, Amadi, don't sound so mysterious. Who is she, if you know her? '

' She's Miss Aduke Olowu.'

' What? Miss Olowu? If it's juju, may it not infect me! ' The sudden change baffled Amadi. ' Why? ' he asked.

' Is that the girl who, I hear, is giving you sleepless nights? ' As Amadi tried to answer Chima went on: ' My friend this is the University of Southern Nigeria and you are a Freshman. Like a chicken transported to a strange environment, you should stand on one leg till you are sure of your ground.

' But I still don't understand.'

Chima looked towards Macaulay Hall as if to make certain that Miss Olowu was not eavesdropping. ' Let me cut the matter neatly like a scarf. That girl is Yoruba, you are Ibo. The twain cannot meet.'

'Do you mean a Yoruba girl and an Ibo boy cannot be friends?'

'I am not speculating. No such thing has happened on the campus of this University since I arrived, and that's about two years now. On the contrary, there have been many woeful failures. Do you know Mr Obi?'

'No,' replied Amadi.

'Mr Obi and Miss Solanke belonged to the same study group of the Student Christian Movement. At a discussion on Christian marriage, he was swept off his feet by her defence of inter-racial and inter-tribal marriages, as the practical demonstration of the truth that in Christ there is no East or West. Then, oaf that he was, he forgot she spoke from the pulpit. Every attempt by some of us to recall him to his senses was like forcing a stream to flow uphill. He learnt his lesson the day he called for her at Oliaku Hall.

'He had seen her clearly from a distance as she entered her room. When the Porter told him she had gone out, he described to him the colour of the dressing-gown she wore as he saw her go into her room.

'"Look, my friend," the Porter said in a low tone, "if na me be you I go go back read my book!"

'"Why?" Obi asked.

'"Your name no be Obi?"

'"Yes" and Obi drew nearer, his pulse quickening in anxiety.

'"Miss Solanke don tell us say any time Obi come ask for am, make we tell am say she no dey for Hall. Make you no tell am na me tell you O! Na only because me I no like de way you dey waste your time come here everyday, das why I tell you de troot."

'After that it was unnecessary to persuade Obi to forget Miss Solanke,' concluded Chima.

'Are you sure Miss Solanke mightn't have done the same thing to a Yoruba man?'

'You're still a Freshman. By the time you've spent some years here you'll think differently. In any case you're engaged to a beautiful young girl at home. You have no need for a serious friend here; all you need is perhaps an occasional fling and this you can get from some other quarters without much effort. All the same, you don't have to take my advice. You are as free as a damsel to develop your breasts where you choose.'

With that Chima mounted his cranky bicycle and rattled off to submit an essay to his Lecturer in European History.

For some seconds Amadi stayed glued to the spot. Then he moved instinctively to Macaulay Hall. Aduke was neither in the Porter's Lodge nor in the adjoining dining room. He walked into the Porter's Lodge and scanned the pages of the Visitors' Book, curious to see the name of the student she had called to see. The entry showed that she was attending a meeting in the Junior Common Room.

'These blasted meetings!'

The Porter thought Amadi spoke to him.

'Dat book na for women students wey enter dis Hall. Which student you wan' see?'

'No one.'

Amadi shut the book and walked out. It was half past six by his watch and he reckoned the meeting would be over by 6.45 to allow the students attending it time for a wash in preparation for formal dinner at 7.30. He decided to wait in the Convocation Hall, two minutes' walk from Macaulay Hall. He could kill time by admiring the bronze head of the Chancellor of the University, the bust of the historical King Jaja of Opobo, and the record-player that undergraduates were not allowed to operate save under the expert eye of the University Accountant, who charged them a bottle of whisky each time he was in attendance. But Amadi was not thinking about any of these as he paced slowly round the rectangular Hall. His mind was weighing Chima's words.

He had a girl at Ezinkwo, his home. Nwakaego Ikwuaju was the most eligible girl at Ezinkwo—beautiful and unspoilt. She had been betrothed to him from childhood, to the knowledge of everyone in the village. His parents, with the co-operation of her own, had done all within their power to train her to become an ideal daughter-in-law. Because of his insistence during his first term in the University, she had recently been sent to a Secondary Modern School from where, after two years, she would proceed to a four-year Higher Elementary Teachers' Training College. No girl at Ezinkwo had ever attained that level of education, but Amadi had insisted that his wife should have nothing less.

He could not forget the experience of their Latin master at school. At the time he chose a wife, he had no idea that he would one day travel to the United Kingdom for further studies. His ideal was a girl with a primary school leaving certificate, for he argued that such a girl would find it easier to accept a husband's authority than a girl with a higher level of education. He lived very happily with his wife before his departure to the United Kingdom. The headaches began after he got back with a degree in Classics. Shortly after his return, the Principal and some other members of the staff called at his house to welcome him home.

'Darling!' he called to his wife, in an attempt to be British.

'Sir!' she answered from the kitchen.

The arrangements for Nwakaego's education would prevent such embarrassing episodes. A girl with a Higher Elementary Certificate would make a wife suitable for even the Vice-Chancellor of a University. But Chima was right—he was not in quest of a wife.

What then did he want with Aduke? An occasional fling, as Chima had described it? As he paced slowly round the Convocation Hall he realised he had never given the matter serious thought, or any thought at all. He had been told about a special part of the University town where 'occasional flings' were readily available for a few shillings. The older women, worn out by the rigours of their profession, would accept even a shilling for 'one trip'. Sometimes they brought their wares to the campus at no additional expense to their customers.

'Money for hand, back na ground!' That was the Ezinkwo description for cheap women. Amadi detested them, and had promised his parents he would avoid them like lepers. None of them could give him the feeling of achievement.

Feeling of achievement. Could that be his reason for wanting Aduke? Nwakaego, his bride-to-be, had been won for him by his parents, and not through his proficiency in the technique of courtship. He nursed the hope that he could win a girl's love all by himself. Aduke provided the opportunity.

What chance had he? From all he had heard, University girls were tough to conquer. In the words of a local band-leader:

> *Dem go make you spend so so money,*
> *Till you fall for ground like Hausa beggar;*
> *But dem give you notin for your money*
> *Only calling you darling when dem need your cheque.*
> *So, mister, when you see dem woman, pick race O!*

To complicate matters, Aduke was Yoruba and he was Ibo. 'It will certainly be an uphill task. But what if I fail? What have I to lose?'

His thoughts were interrupted by the students emerging from Macaulay Hall in twos and threes. He positioned himself at a vantage point in front of the Convocation Hall, ready to intercept Aduke as she made her way to Oliaku Hall. As he was composing his opening sentence she appeared from the Porter's Lodge, accompanied by a male undergraduate. They spoke Yoruba so he could not understand what they were discussing. Aduke took no notice of him as she walked past, deeply engaged in conversation with her escort, who beamed as if he had won first prize in the Government Lotteries.

'Could it be that Chima is right and I am being naive beyond words?'

2

It was at the Vice-Chancellor's traditional address to Freshmen that Amadi was first drawn to Aduke. That was five months ago, one evening early in October. Amadi had stepped into the University Auditorium feeling pleased with himself in his light blue nylon shirt, dark grey woollen trousers, shining black shoes, and the Old Boys' tie of his secondary school. He knew that, but for the tie, he was in the outfit for which the Nigerian undergraduate was widely known; the outfit which, complete with University tie, a walking-stick and an empty pipe, had earned him the nick-name of 'Gay Adder'. He had no jacket because he had been advised to save up the money for a complete suit until he arrived on the campus, where he would find innumerable tailors with overseas diplomas.

The Auditorium was virtually full by the time he came in. The few vacant seats were in the front rows where he disliked sitting. Luckily he spotted a vacant seat in the middle of the hall and squeezed his way to it, walking on the balls of his feet to minimise the noise made by the studded leather soles of his shoes. Many eyes followed him. The eyes turned away as he sat down; the seat he occupied must obviously have been a centre of attraction. Five girls sat on the right, separated by his chair from the male students on the left.

He had never seen anything like the Auditorium. The seats were immovable and were fitted with very comfortable rubber cushions. He was struck by the ingenious way in which ash trays were fixed on these seats. The white man's smoking habits make him provide ash trays almost everywhere, he reflected. The ceiling was very attractive, with electric bulbs that appeared buried in asbestos. Between the rows of numbered seats and the stage was a grand piano,

14

placed within the enclosure for an orchestra. The stage was edged with footlights, overhead were lamps of diverse colours and in the background hung heavy curtains. There was nothing on the bare stage to suggest those wonderful scenes pictured in the University Journal, but he hoped before long he would see the University Players in full swing.

His wandering eyes were called to order by the entry of the Vice-Chancellor in black gown and mortar board; all rose and stood in respectful silence, resuming their seats at a signal from him. When his address began many were surprised that a European could speak without a script.

' It gives me great pleasure to welcome you to this University,' the Vice-Chancellor said.

'. . . The University is a corporate body . . . All its members, senior and junior, have one common aim— the quest for Truth . . .'

Amadi felt something soft and cold on his elbow and he recoiled as if he had touched an electric fish. He then remembered he was sitting next to a girl and wished he had not moved his arm. While the Vice-Chancellor spoke he tried unobtrusively for another touch, but the girl's arms were now securely folded.

'. . . University Professors are very interesting when you get to know them. They are often associated with absent-mindedness. One eminent Professor of Political Science whom I know very well was once complaining bitterly to his class about irresponsible speakers who never turned up when they were supposed to. The previous evening, he said, he had wasted thirty good minutes in Trafalgar Square in the midst of a huge crowd waiting for a Professor who was to have given a public lecture under the auspices of the Movement for Colonial Freedom. The speaker failed to show up and the angry crowd refused to listen to a substitute speaker.

' One of his students who had also been there, held up his arm.

' " But, sir, the lecture was to have been delivered by you! "

' The Professor nervously searched for his diary . . .'

The joke sent everybody into roars of laughter. Amadi

turned towards the unknown girl, to share the joke with her. She returned the glance, also laughing. He was surprised at her beauty and her youth, having come to the University expecting to see only old and ugly women who needed University degrees to enhance their chances of getting husbands.

She drifted away from him at the end of the address, without giving him a chance to ask her name.

'If the animal escapes today, tomorrow is still hunting day!' He was determined to find out more about her. By the time they met a second time he had discovered that she was Miss Aduke Olowu, and that she was hoping to study History at the University.

Unforeseen difficulties, however, at the beginning of his first term at the University left him no time for affairs of the heart. He had arrived at the campus determined to register for the Honours course in English.

His choice had been influenced by the addition to the staff of his school of a young Cambridge graduate, Mr Ola, whose 'Cambridge manners' had swept Amadi and many other boys off their feet. Although Mr Ola was a Nigerian and his hair was always cut short, he had a habit of stroking his hair backwards as if to keep the flowing locks in order. Within a short while he had revolutionised pronunciation in the whole school. Even the way he gave orders to the school at Saturday morning parades appeared special. And so, in spite of his excellent performances in Physics, Chemistry and Biology, Amadi arrived at the University determined to study English like his hero, Mr Ola.

The shock came when he failed the selection examination set by the Department of English. The Professor of English refused to accept his plea that it had been his life ambition to study English, and that he could not think of any other subject he could study. All the sympathy he received was the permission to re-sit the selection examination at the beginning of the following academic year, in competition with Freshmen. This he could not accept.

For some time he brooded over his failure to read English.

The Professor of English had been very curt with him when they had met that morning. His countenance, never very inviting, and the way he literally brushed Amadi aside, had vaporized the words in Amadi's mouth. He could not understand why a person's life ambition should be thwarted by one isolated test, details of which were only vaguely stated beforehand.

He went to Chima for advice. Should he go and see the Professor in his house?

'Don't waste your time,' Chima counselled. 'Professor Geoffreys is a negrophobist. He simply doesn't believe that any African understands the English language.'

'But suppose I beg him to allow me to join the class for a term, at the end of which I could be rejected if I fail to make the grade?' Amadi asked.

'You don't know the man you're dealing with,' said Chima, shaking his head. 'Whoever heard of anyone visiting Professor Geoffreys in his house? Even students who used to cycle to his house to hand in their essays have stopped doing so. Why? Because to him they might just as well be newspaper boys coming to slip the *Daily Times* under the door. You should thank your stars that you were not selected for the course. How many of his students ever graduate?'

Amadi was looking into space, and Chima went on.

'All his students think in terms of a Third Class degree; that is if they pass at all. We hear he got a Lower Second in his time, and naturally he wouldn't be happy to see any one under him get a higher class degree than himself—it would be an acknowledgement that the student had a superior brain. Can you believe that one student whom he failed in the Intermediate later went to Cambridge where he made a Second Upper in English? Don't waste your time with him; it will merely heighten his contempt for Africans. Have no fear, we shall teach him a lesson when Nigeria attains independence.'

Amadi walked away, disappointed. The future of Professor Geoffreys in an independent Nigeria did not interest him. His immediate concern was that he could not read English Honours like Mr Ola.

Then an idea struck him. If he could not read what he had dreamed of reading, why not revert to the course his people wanted him to take? Medicine was in every person's mouth at home. His parents had dreamed of the day their son would be a doctor, the first doctor produced by Ezinkwo town. They had imagined how he would get all the money that went to those merciless and greedy doctors who came from Onitsha every Afo market day. His mother dreamed of the day that everyone would call her, *Nne dokita:* mother of a doctor, of the day when headache, toothache and backache would disappear from their home. When they were approached for financial assistance, the Ezinkwo Improvement League had expressed a preference for Medicine. He himself had never wished for Medicine as a career, what with his disgust for chronic ulcers and his fear of dead bodies. But since he could not read the subject of his choice, he might as well read Medicine. Doctors were men of consequence in society.

At ten o'clock the following morning he was in the office of the Academic Registrar.

' What's your trouble? ' asked the Academic Registrar lifting his eyes from his draft, and taking off his glasses with considerable ceremony.

' It's about my course, sir,' answered Amadi.

The telephone rang.

' Just a minute. Sit down, young man, while I take this call.'

Amadi sank into the large armchair.

' Hullo . . . speaking . . . No, I haven't yet seen anyone of that name. I agree with you that we ought to adopt a firm attitude about these constant demands for changes of courses or we shall never get anywhere . . . Yes . . . The matter has already been put up to the Senate and they hold the same view . . . Very well, I shall certainly discourage any students who approach me . . . Yes . . . I think their problem is that they think everyone is born an Honours student . . . Right you are . . . 'bye.'

The Academic Registrar made a few notes on his scribbling pad, which gave Amadi time to collect himself. He concluded that it must have been Professor Geoffreys on the telephone talking about him and he decided to have nothing more to do with English.

'Now, young man, what can I do for you?'

'It's about my course.'

'What about your course?' asked the Academic Registrar. 'Are you one of those men who think they must obtain an Honours degree?'

'Not quite, Sir,' Amadi replied evasively. 'I want to read Medicine.'

'And you were admitted for Agriculture or Science?' asked the Academic Registrar, almost adding 'I've heard that one before'.

'No, I was admitted for an Arts degree.'

'Arts! And you want to read Medicine?'

'Yes, sir.'

The Academic Registrar put on his glasses and took a closer look at him.

'Why do you sound so confident?'

'I had a good record in Physics, Chemistry and Biology at school. Some of my classmates who were no better than me have been admitted for Medicine.'

The Academic Registrar adopted a more serious attitude.

'My son, between you and me and this table, I would say —read whatever you think you can read. After all, there's a lot to be said for reading a subject one loves. I was myself compelled to read Medicine because Medicine was in our family—my father, my mother, my grandfather were all doctors, and I, as the eldest son, was also expected to qualify as a doctor. I forced myself to take the course for a year, and then decided to give it up and damn the consequences. Today, I don't regret that I didn't qualify as a doctor, and I'm eternally happy that I read the subject of my choice.'

Amadi lifted his eyes, buoyed up with hope.

'But, of course, if one considers it from the other angle, from the point of view of Heads of Departments, one will agree that frequent changes of subjects and courses make serious planning impossible. The Professor of English has just spoken to me over the phone about students who have been pestering his life lately because he refused to be dictated to by them.'

The barometer fell.

'And there's also the question of your sponsors, who have guaranteed your fees on the understanding that you would pursue an Arts degree course. I don't know whether they would agree to sponsor you for Medicine, which is a longer and much more expensive course.'

'They will,' cut in Amadi. 'In fact, they wanted me to read Medicine.'

The Academic Registrar again removed his glasses and paused for thought, biting his pencil in the process. 'Well, my son, the decision is not mine to take. Send me a formal application for a change of course. It might strengthen your case if you attach to it a written undertaking from your sponsors that they are willing to sponsor you for Medicine. I promise to present your application to the appropriate committee, but that is the only promise I am making. By the way, what's your name?'

Amadi Chukwuka, Sir.'

'How do you spell it?' He wrote down the name as Amadi spelt it.

It was a hopeful Amadi that walked out of the Academic Registrar's Office. At last he had found a man who understood his difficulties, having at one time had a similar experience. How could he get the letter from his sponsors in the quickest possible time? Letters usually took about a week to get to Ezinkwo, and telegrams sometimes longer, and the people at home might not appreciate the urgency of the matter if he merely sent them a letter.

The best thing to do was to dash home and bring back the letter himself. He ruled out discussing the matter with Chima this time, as he feared Chima would discover some snags and dissuade him from putting his plan into action.

It was fairly easy to obtain an exeat for four days.

As soon as he arrived home, he and his father went to see the Chairman of the Improvement League. To many anxious enquiries from people they met on the way, Amadi replied that he had merely come home to collect some books and

clothes he had forgotten. The Chairman, who was a prominent carpenter in the town, was most sympathetic. He
thought, in view of the urgency of the matter, that there was
no need to summon a meeting of the League before writing
the letter. He would see the Secretary that night, and ask
him to cycle to Amagu, six miles away, and get the Pastor's
clerk there to type the letter for them.

Everything worked out well and Amadi returned to the
University late on the fourth day, armed with a letter addressed
to the Academic Registrar, which read:

Sir,

At an emergency meeting of the Ezinkwo Improvement
League it was decided that we should communicate
directly with you on our proposal to train Amadi Chukwuka Esquire, in Medicine. He is already at your
University.

Our health condition is very poor, ignorance is rampant,
the standard of education exceptionally low. We believe
that the only man who can draw the attention of our
people from oracles, etc. as a means of curing illness is
an indigenous doctor who can work among the people.
The only person qualified to become a doctor in the
whole town is Amadi Chukwuka Esquire, as he is the only
son of the town who has been through a secondary school.
We believe that he will serve us satisfactorily.

We are prepared to be responsible for the cost of his
training in your University, and we pray and trust that
you will help us. Amadi has already told us of your
kindness to him for which we express sincere gratitude.
There is a proverb which says that the chicken can never
forget the person who plucks the feathers of its tail during
the rainy season.

The letter was signed by the President and the Secretary
of the Ezinkwo Improvement League.

Two weeks passed, during which Amadi was kept in
suspense.

Then one day, when he returned to his room after lunch, he
found a brown envelope stuck to the number plate on his

door. With trembling fingers and hungry eyes he tore open the envelope.

Mr A. Chukwuka,
Niger Hall

Dear Mr Chukwuka,

I refer to your recent application for a transfer from the Faculty of Arts to the Faculty of Medicine. The Committee of Deans at its last meeting went into the matter very carefully, particularly in the light of the supporting letter from your sponsors. However, it ruled, with the deepest regret, that it would not depart from its earlier decision that no transfer from other Faculties to the Faculty of Medicine should be permitted during the current academic year, otherwise it would be creating a dangerous precedent.

The Committee noted that you have been attending lectures in the Faculty of Science, possibly in anticipation of its decision. I have therefore been requested to warn you that you must now revert to the History Honours course, to which the Committee was informed you had been offered admission.

Yours sincerely,

Academic Registrar

And so Amadi became a History Honours student and found himself in Aduke's class. He had not applied to read History, neither did he sit the qualifying test. He did not know who told the Committee of Deans that he had been admitted to the course, and he had no intention of finding out. When at the end of the first term the History Department discovered that he should not have been in the Honours class, it was difficult to know where to lay the blame. The Professor of History reluctantly agreed to give him a trial, on the understanding that he would be rejected if he made a poor showing during the year, especially at the sessional examinations.

3

The last Saturday of the academic year was to be a special day. A special election of the Students' Union was to be held—between eight in the morning and five in the evening—to elect a delegate to represent the Union at an international conference at Leiden in Holland, during August. Amadi looked forward to the election—his first opportunity to exercise a franchise, all Freshmen having been denied the privilege of voting at the last Students' Representative Council elections in October because, at that time, they had not matriculated. A Students' Union End-of-year Dance was to follow at ten o'clock. Amadi considered this the golden opportunity to establish his claim over Aduke beyond dispute. He bought a double ticket for the dance, in the hope that she would go with him. This would proclaim him her ' driver ', any other student attempting to befriend her after that would be contravening accepted ' traffic regulations '.

The elections proved to be a thrilling experience for him. It was a straight fight between Ezenagu, a second-year History Honours student and popular crowd-puller, and Obafemi, a Freshman medical student.

' Gentlemen of Niger Hall, lend me your knives and forks ! '

There was a peal of laughter in the dining hall, and even though a few diners who sat near the high table threw knives and forks at Ezenagu, the Hall decided to give him a hearing.

' I have not come here to promise all final year students first class examination results. That would be promising the impossible and, as a famous French historian once said, to promise what is impossible is to deceive the world.'

There was loud applause, mingled with shouts of 'Great !',

' *Oyibo!* ', ' Up, Cock Robin! ', ' *Supa!* ', and ' *Akwukwo!*'.

A supporter jingled the dining-hall bell and the noise subsided. Ezenagu continued:

' All I ask is that you judge me by my past performances. My record of selfless service to the Union is my open testimonial.'

' What service have you rendered the Union, you braggart? You think you can come here to show us that you are studying the French Revolution which we all mastered in the Primary School, you Cock Robin! '

The questioner would not wait for an answer. He had had his supper and did not want a second course. Some students walked out with him. The bell jingled, and Ezenagu raised his voice.

' I did not want to bore you by recounting the various capacities in which I have served the Union. But since I have been challenged to name them, I shall be telegraphic. Who, as Union Sports Secretary, persuaded the University authorities to raise the budget for sports? Who spearheaded the move by the Students' Representative which has now resulted in the abolition of residence in that place of outer darkness called the Transit Campus? And if I may come nearer home, who, as Minister of Food in this great Hall, this premier Hall, this Hall of Gentlemen, called a halt to the indignities of the self-service system? '

' Great! Great! Vote for Ezenagu! ' The shout was spontaneous. The Hall had felt very strongly about the self-service system. The undergraduates considered it degrading to have to carry their food in trays from the service counter to the dining tables. Three Hall Committees had been overthrown for failing to stop the obnoxious system. Ezenagu succeeded where others had failed, and his popularity transcended the boundaries of Niger Hall, especially as he had achieved this in his Freshman year.

He was beaming as he held up his right hand like a preacher pronouncing the benediction on a loyal flock. ' I do not intend to make a long speech because it is unnecessary. I only wish to remind you that Ezenagu is, and will always remain, a loyal Nigerite.'

24

'Up Niger! Up Ezenagu!' His supporters carried him shoulder high to another Hall.

Obafemi was busy campaigning in another part of the huge campus. The Freshmen decided to stand solidly behind him, in protest against the treatment they had received during the previous Students' Representative Council elections. Obafemi had not served the Union in any official capacity, but he had quickly established himself as the best soccer centre forward the University had seen for years. His legs were sharp, as the students say, and his speed with the ball had earned him the nickname of 'Local Sputnik'. He exploited his popularity in soccer to the full. One of his posters read:

DO YOU KNOW YOU CAN LAUNCH YOUR OWN SPUTNIK?
JUST PICK UP A BALLOT PAPER. MARK X AGAINST
YOUR OWN SPUTNIK (OBAFEMI). SQUEEZE IT INTO THE
ROCKET (BALLOT BOX). YOUR SPUTNIK IS SURE TO
LAND IN LEIDEN AT THE APPOINTED TIME. A TRIAL
WILL CONVINCE YOU.

The Freshmen knew they needed every trick of propaganda and originality if Obafemi was to beat a popular candidate like Ezenagu. They added a new chapter to the history of Students' Union elections by hiring the popular Moonlight Orchestra to join their campaign team as it toured the various Halls of Residence.

The performance for each Hall was the same. The orchestra started off with the popular highlife: *Bonsue*. Everybody— Obafemi and his supporters, orchestra and all—twisted and wriggled on the tops of the dining tables to the enchanting tune. Stewards and cooks joined in the infectious dance.

'Ladies and Gentlemen—I am particularly pleased to see that every member of Oliaku Hall supports me . . .'

'Great! Up, Sputnik! Down Ezenagu! . . .'

'Ladies and Gentlemen! I feel flattered by the support you have all given me. Speech making is the prerogative of Cock Robins such as my honourable opponent. I believe in quick action, that's why goalkeepers hate me. The Moonlight Orchestra will play a special composition after which I invite you all to the courtyard of this great Hall for a final treat.'

Further shouts died away as the orchestra played a special calypso recounting Sputnik's brilliant performances in various soccer matches. It was adapted from the popular calypso written for Nigeria's World Featherweight Boxing Champion. The excited dancers joined the orchestra in singing the chorus:

' Local Sputnik; shoot them, 'Femi, don't you stop! '

At the end of it, Obafemi was carried shoulder high to the open courtyard. His Terylene suit was thoroughly soaked. He wiped some of the sweat off his brow with his fingers as he spoke:

' Ladies and Gentlemen! Tomorrow is *the* Day, Sputnik Day, *my* Day! I ask only one little favour of you all. Tomorrow morning take a stroll to your Porter's Lodge. Pick up a ballot paper. Mark X against my name. Fold the paper like this, and drop it into the ballot box. Then watch what happens.'

A ball of fire shot into the air from a safe distance, breaking up into smaller balls like a fountain shooting up particles of water in diverse colours. The fireworks were perfectly timed.

' That's your Sputnik flying to Leiden! '

4

' Obafemi was luckier than he deserved,' observed Chima.

' Where's the luck in being defeated, especially after such a vigorous campaign? ' asked Amadi.

' Campaign my yash! You Freshmen think we're truck pushers and Ochanja market women, to be swept off our feet by cheap highlife. Who knows Obafemi? He plays soccer well, so he thinks everybody must know him. How many students watch soccer matches? And then the childish emphasis on Sputnik, as if the Sputnik Athletic Club is not always last in every competition, with millipedes as their

26

sprinters! He should count himself lucky to be beaten by only ninety-five votes. It would have been tragic to elect as our representative one of those peacocks called medical students who always claim to be too busy to attend any meeting. By the way, what time do you make it? '

' 9.15.'

' Hurrah, the Tower clock appears to be accurate today.'

' Are you sure it's moving? '

' We'll soon see. The dance doesn't begin till ten. We could kill time by watching the clock.'

' Architects must be queer people,' Amadi remarked. ' Imagine fixing clocks on the two sides of the Tower where they are least necessary and leaving off the side facing the University Drive, the one side where a clock is indispensable.' When Chima failed to make any comments Amadi decided to modify his views: ' It's a lovely Tower, though.'

' That may be so, but what is the purpose in spending thousands of pounds on a skyscraper whose main function is to house lavatories. Yet whenever we ask for better food we are told there's no money.'

They walked slowly up and down the car park, casting anxious glances each time they saw a vehicle approaching, to see whether it was the bus carrying the nurses. Chima was fixed up. His regular girl friend was coming in the bus. Amadi hoped that Chima's friend might bring another girl, failing that he might pounce on one of the uncommitted nurses who, he heard, often turned up for University dances.

Shortly after casting his vote he had gone to Oliaku Hall to ask Aduke to accompany him to the dance. The Porter told him she was not in the Hall. After lunch he had again gone in quest of her.

' Is Miss Olowu in? '

The Porter sized him up. ' Yes.'

The Porter broke the short pause which followed: ' You want make I call am for you? '

' Er . . ., not exactly; no.'

Many thoughts were going through Amadi's mind. 'How should I put the question to her? Suppose she refuses, shall I have the face to see her again? Would it be wise to ask her at the Porter's Lodge, in the presence of the Porter and perhaps any passer-by? No, it would be better to ask the Porter to take me to her room. Then only the two of us would be involved, and a refusal would be easier to bear. But the regulations require me to give my name to the Porter and then wait for him to check from her whether she wishes to see me. I am sure she will not refuse to see me. On more than one occasion she has asked me whether I ever visit Oliaku Hall, no doubt hoping I would call on her some day. I could begin by telling her that I called casually and naturally thought I should say hello to her. I need not introduce the dance until . . . '

A car stopped in front of the Porter's Lodge and a young man in spotless white lace *agbada* breezed in.

' Is Miss Aduke Olowu in? '

' Yes, sir,' replied the Porter, bubbling over with civility.

' Please tell her that 'Kunle is waiting in the car for her.'

The Porter looked at Amadi as if to say ' Well, what say you? ' And Amadi, waking from his day dream, nodded as the Porter went away.

Amadi's first impulse was to hold his ground. The situation would be ideal for testing Aduke's feelings for him. But the sight of her stepping out of her room almost as soon as the Porter knocked on the door unnerved him. She must have been waiting for 'Kunle. The man must be in Government Service since he owned a car. His name was obviously a Yoruba one. What chances had Amadi? He might as well hope to pull out the whiskers of a wide-awake and hungry lion. Before Aduke came near enough to recognise him, he had gone.

He hoped for the best as he and Chima talked away the time at the University car park, waiting for the arrival of the nurses. After his experience at a night club in town he had resolved never to attend another dance without a dancing partner of his own. He had accompanied a few friends to the Club one day after listening to the advice of their Senior Lecturer in History, who thought it was not out of place for a student, after a hard week's work in History, to visit a night club on a Saturday night and forget all about History for a while.

28

As he and his friends entered the night club the band was playing *Rapukwam na twelve akugo*, a popular highlife. There were coloured lights, round tables and steel chairs. In a specially constructed stand was the orchestra—a heterogeneous collection of amateurs. They soon finished the highlife and began tuning their instruments to start the next piece.

At one end of the garden was a couple who looked as incompatible as a man and a woman could look. The girl was a young Nigerian, rather attractive. The man was a huge white who had well near exhausted his quota of three score and ten years. His cheeks were hollow, and it would have been interesting to count his teeth. His dental formula, thought Amadi, must be similar to that of the town crier in his home village. The girl threw her arm round the man and the word ' darling ' fell from her mouth. The man contrived a smile.

More people came in and more drinks passed round, whisky, Star beer, Samson stout, Tango, Coca-Cola, gin, brandy . . .

The orchestra came alive again, after ten minutes spent in tuning their instruments. They were playing another highlife. The huge toothless white and the Nigerian girl were on the floor, the girl out in front and moving well and the huge man copying her movements awkwardly from the rear. There were other couples dancing. Amadi noticed three women sitting alone behind him. The way men meandered away from them reminded him of the Biblical story of the labourers who stood idle in the market-place, for no one would hire them. The women had thin, pencilled eyebrows which extended down to their cheeks, and dusty red lipstick. And they smoked like candles.

' I'll ask one of those dames for a dance,' Amadi told his companions.

' By all means. Wish you luck.'

The woman heaved a sigh, adjusted her rubber brassière and rose to dance with him.

" How are you enjoying the evening?' he asked.

' Small, small.'

The highlife was over. Immediately the band began the

only waltz of the night. A waltz being Amadi's favourite, he asked his partner for another dance.

' I no dey dance dis kind.'

He was disappointed, but had to take her back to her seat.

' Thank you for the wonderful time,' he said with a forced smile.

' You no go buy me sometin' make I drink? '

The request shocked him, not only because it came from an unknown lady but also because he had not come prepared for such expensive acts of generosity. He decided not to hear the request, and walked off slowly but with dignity.

' My frien', you dey go because I say make you buy me stout? '

' Just a minute,' was all he could reply as he walked away.

A quarter of an hour later he tried another girl at the far end of the hall.

' Bo,' she sighed as he asked her for a dance, ' I want to took some beer first.'

' Took on! ' he replied spontaneously, and walked away, disgusted but amused by his logical reply. A bottle of beer per dance! Was he a money doubler? His two companions had been more successful, and were so attached to their new-won partners that they told him he could return to the University whenever he chose; they would follow later. As he moved towards the door, he noticed the toothless white and the Nigerian girl were still in their corner. This time they were closer together. Their lips met. They kissed. The girl stroked the man's neck; the man pressed her tight. Amadi swallowed hard and walked out into the starry night, swearing he would never attend another dance without a decent partner.

' Sure enough, that's the bus,' shouted Chima.

Amadi's heart beat faster. Would he have any luck, with such a long queue of undergraduates waiting for the nurses ? He looked himself over in his mind's eye. In his dark grey suit (with a single-button jacket) made by the famous Olu with the first class London diploma, he was confident he could hold his own.

The bus came to a halt and the nurses jumped down. The undergraduates, in their well-ironed suits and shining black shoes, hands in pockets, formed a ravenous guard of honour for the 'organic buses' as the girls were nicknamed. The guard of honour broke off in confusion as those of its members who knew the nurses joined the onward drift, hand in hand with their partners for the night. Chima left Amadi without even a cold farewell, and chatted off non-stop in Ibo with Miss Osakwe as they walked together towards the gate. Amadi's confidence walked away with Chima. His body followed involuntarily for a while, but when his conspicuous efforts at clearing his throat failed to attract the least attention from Chima he turned off to the left as if he was making for the Students' Centre.

'Well, that's that!' A lot went into that sentence: an unforeseen and unhappy end to days of intensive mental preparation; a sudden realisation that he was backboneless, as the students would describe it, and lacked the courage to 'attack' a girl he had not previously been introduced to; a feeling too that he was deliberately shutting his eyes to the obvious signs from Providence warning him to steer clear of Aduke.

'It serves you right!' one voice told him. 'Imagine carrying an elephant on your head and attempting to pick up little crickets with your toes!'

'I only wanted to take Aduke to the dance,' he told himself rather loudly, in an effort to counteract the inner voice. 'There's nothing wrong in that. In case there is, I now sacrifice my seven and sixpenny ticket and retire to bed.'

After what had been a very hectic day for every Freshman, he found his Vono bed waiting to receive him.

'Hey, Mr Chukwuka, what are you doing in pyjamas when there's hot music in the Convocation Hall?' Obafemi dragged him up from his bed.

'*Oga*, I feel worn out, and my eyelids are falling in love with each other,' lied Amadi. 'It has been a hectic day for us, as you know.'

'Come on, man, if you are feeling worn out and sleepy, what about me? But I'd rather put ground alligator pepper under my eyelids than go to bed. Ezenagu must not think too much of his victory. And I want all my supporters to come with me. So, off with your pyjamas. If you're broke, I'll square you up.'

' In actual fact I possess a double ticket.'

' Then what's your headache! There'll be girls in super-abundance—a contingent from the Nursing School, two bus loads from Mount Sinai, many free-lancers from the night clubs and the Latin quarters—wanting partners. And of course Miss Olowu and your Oliaku Hall friends. It won't cost you more than a bottle of Fanta for the whole night if you pick your partner well.'

Amadi woke up at eleven o'clock next morning with an empty stomach and a terrible hangover. He had never drunk gin in his life except for the little shot of *aka mere* he stole from his father's bottle while in Standard Five. His head hammered the way it did when, in his first year in the Secondary School, a thick-set student nicknamed Ugepian Bullet, acting on the instructions of a prefect, gave him a crack on the head with his knuckles. He tried to think. The gin, in spite of the present hangover, had done him some good. It had knocked off the initial shyness, and made him imper-vious to rudeness from the girls who did not want to dance with him. It even made him attempt a tango, and also made him abandon it promptly in the interest of his partner's shin bones.

Above all, the gin had put words into his mouth when he met Aduke. He saw her dancing past him at an excuse-me-dance and had made for her without apology.

' At last! '

' What's that? ' asked Aduke, dancing some complicated movements, with the shoulders and the waist, at arm's length but looking at him.

' You don't know how frantically I have searched for you all over the Hall.' Amadi looked her straight in the face.

' Oh, is that so? ' She revolved on her left foot and danced in a forward direction, backing him.

Amadi was not prepared to be put off. He took a few

long strides, tried a beautiful spin turn and was again in front of her.

'. . . and now that I have found you, someone else is coming for you.'

'Who's that? I'm fed up with this idea of passing from hand to hand.'

As she said this, she clung to him and turned her face away from the direction of her new dancing partner.

Chima heard her, he cast a castigating glance towards Amadi and changed direction like a millipede when its feelers encounter an obstacle.

'Thank goodness!' The words were hardly out of her mouth when the band stopped. Amadi held on to her, waiting for the band to strike up another highlife.

'Thank you, thank you, thank you, ladies and gentlemen! There will be a short interval of fifteen minutes, to give ladies and gentlemen some breathing space, and time to . . . you know what I mean!' The Master of Ceremonies was in his usual light-hearted mood. 'And I have been asked to announce that the bar is still inexhaustible!'

Amadi sat up on his bed, leaned forward, pressed his right arm on his chest and succeeded in preventing the gin and other contents of his inside from jumping out. He wiped his mouth; it had too much salt in it. He lay flat on his back, to see whether sleep would come to his rescue. No more sleep for him. His head knocked even harder, as if people were stampeding on it, dancing ' *Nzogbu! Enyi mba enyi!* '

Suddenly he shot up from his bed and emptied the contents of his stomach on the floor. He looked at the watery mess. The smell of the gin was unmistakable. He loathed the sight and looked round for a rag to mop it up.

All the same the gin had worked to his advantage last night. During the interval he had been able to tell Aduke how he admired her and how he had longed to tell her so. He had also told her about the double ticket he had bought for the dance, and learnt that 'Kunle was the husband of a school friend of hers and that he had called to take her to the

3   33

hospital to see his wife and their first child, born the previous day.

How did it all end? He could not remember now.

He threw the rag, wet with the mess into the small bucket he used as a waste paper basket.

Someone knocked on the door. He ignored the knock. Whoever it was should go back the way he came. A second knock. The door opened slowly.

' Miss Olowu! '

Aduke pulled out the key from the Yale lock and banged the door. ' I see you forgot to remove your key from the door before you slept last night, or have you been out this morning? '

Amadi opened his mouth and shut it again. He looked at his messy fingers and at the floor. His head hammered.

'So, you've got rid of it, eh? Should do you some good. I saw you were in bad shape last night, that's why I decided to accompany you as far as your Porter's Lodge before I went to my Hall.'

Amadi stood up. ' Do you mean you followed me to my Hall last night? You don't mean it! ' As he said this, he approached her.

She was not very inviting. ' I would advise you to get to the bathroom first. And perhaps you could bring some drinking water with you in the flask after you have had a bath. I brought some codeine tablets for you in case you needed them.'

He put on his colourful dressing-gown and carrying a flask under his arm left the room.

Aduke made his bed, sat on his reading chair, and picked up Chinua Achebe's *Things Fall Apart*.

5

The smallness of Ezinkwo was more glaring than ever to Amadi after the year he had spent in the enormous University town. Instead of the four-storeyed and impressive buildings of the campus he saw now, on his arrival home for the long vacation, houses with thatched roofs. Even the double-storeyed house belonging to the Chairman of the Improvement League —the only one of its type in the town and generally acclaimed as the most magnificent house within a radius of ten miles —lost its importance; he disliked the prominence given to the staircase and the ill-advised choice of colours.

But home was home. The University town had skyscrapers, it had magnificent buildings like the University Hospital and the Government Buildings. The buildings on the University Campus were both handsome and modern. The view Amadi once had from the top of the University Tower was a most impressive one, houses spreading out in each direction almost as far as the eye could see. But the University town could not mean the same to him as Ezinkwo where he belonged.

Nothing in the University town could compare with the welcome he received the day he arrived for the long vacation. It was Nkwo market day, and the market was full when *No Telephone To Heaven*, the lorry he had boarded, creaked to a halt in front of the market. The Postal Agency had closed for the day, but the Postal Agent was sharing palm wine with six men of his age group, on the verandah of the building which was on the side of the road facing the market.

' *Ewo!* It is Amadi! ' shouted a seamstress whose shed was nearest the lorry, as Amadi stepped off it.

'Oh yes O! It's Amadi, son of Mazi Onuzulike Chukwuka!' The shout echoed through the market and everybody momentarily suspended their higgling and haggling, stretching their necks to see the new arrival. Then came a rush towards Amadi. The women embraced him, the men shook hands with him, the girls greeted him.

'What of Mama Amadi?' enquired some women.

'I am sure she did not come to the market, otherwise she should be here now,' put in one of them, as her eyes searched the area in an effort to pick out Amadi's mother.

'She told me she would not come to the market today, as she wanted to cook food for Amadi. This came from a neighbour, with the air of someone in possession of confidential information.

'Mr Man!' shouted the lorry conductor. 'Don't waste our time. All your load don correct?' Amadi dragged out his luggage and the carton containing his books, checked through the list in his Farmers' Diary and waved the lorry off.

He did not have to look for *onye bulu*, as porters were called at Onitsha. Before he knew what was happening, volunteers had shared his suitcases and carton of books and were already taking them to his father's house.

'Amadi, come and have some palm wine,' offered one of the men as he approached the Postal Agency.

'Thank sirs,' replied Amadi in the village style.

'Didn't I tell you!' whispered the old man who sat next to the Postal Agent. 'You think somebody from University can drink our palm wine?' Like most uneducated people at Ezinkwo, he pronounced University as if it were 'lilivasity'.

'Amadi *anata*, oyo—yo! Amadi *anata*, oyo—yo!' His younger brothers and sisters sped towards him shouting. He balanced his feet firmly on the ground as each one of them jumped up at him. His mother ran well behind the children, as first of all she had to wash her hands and face and put on her *afe itepu* before going to meet her darling son.

After hugging him three times she stood back to size him up.

'Your father keeps arguing with me that you will one day grow fat. Didn't you say they give you eggs and cow's milk there? Eating this *pilipili* white man's food is like eating *agidi*: you think you are satisfied but in one breath everything disappears with the urine.' In spite of this characteristic

36

concern for Amadi's stature, evidence of a mother's pride in her beloved son was clearly written on her face.

This made Amadi feel that he mattered, and that he was not just a Freshman in a large University, itself a tiny part of an enormous city. He knew the University town was not aware of his absence, any more than Otu Onicha would feel the effect even if a whole town decided to boycott it.

Later in the evening, his father returned from the farm. Even he was excited. He shook hands with his son and asked him a series of questions about his Vice-Chancellor, his fellow students, about that white man who had tried his best to help him read Medicine, about his studies.

'Chiebonam!' he called.

'Sir!' Chiebonam answered from the kitchen where she was helping her mother with Amadi's supper.

'Bring that pot of palm wine which Nwakaego's father sent us in the morning.'

The pot was placed in the centre of the visitors who had come to welcome Amadi home.

'I hear that place is wonderful,' put in one of the old men, as he blew off some foreign matter and excess foam from the top of his cup of wine. 'The day Chinwuba returned from there he had no mouth to tell the story. One thing I have not been able to believe is that everybody, including labourers, goes to market in cars. My son, is that one true?'

'I hear books climb on top of each other there. Chinwuba said there was one book which two well-fed people could not carry. Is that true?'

There were many other questions. Mazi Onuzulike Chukwuka smiled happily and proudly as he watched his son answer every question. He was the lucky man in the town, with a son in the University. When Amadi's mother came from the kitchen to drag her son away for a warm bath and a meal, some of the men asked her whether she was competent to prepare a meal for him.

'He is my son,' she replied with pride. 'Even if he goes to England and returns home, he must eat my bitterleaf soup.'

'There is nothing like food cooked by somebody's mother,'

observed one of the men. 'That is why our people say that no person can ever accept that his mother's soup is sour.'

Amadi's first engagement after his arrival at Ezinkwo was to call on the families which had been bereaved during his absence from home. His mother had given him the up-to-date list. He had always regarded this as an unpleasant assignment, and often chose to go in the company of an elder person who would introduce the topic—even though he disliked accompanying elderly women. The way they chatted and laughed merrily on the way, burst into tears as soon as they entered the house, and dried the tears after a few sobs, seemed somehow insincere to him. What surprised him was that the tears were genuine tears and flowed down the cheeks in liberal quantities. All the women needed was a little consolation, someone to tell them 'stop crying!', and the rain clouds would clear.

There was no one to accompany Amadi; if it had been around Christmas time he could have had the company of some teachers or traders who usually came home for the Christmas festivities.

The first house he called at was that of the late Nwankwo Nwafor, as this one was the nearest to their home and it would have been improper to visit more distant houses first. The late Nwankwo Nwafor was not a man of consequence. He was a lazy farmer, the kind of farmer who could not produce enough to feed himself. Each year it was either the yam beetles or the bush fowls that ate up his fine yams. When there were no beetles and bush fowls he complained of a special yam disease known at Ezinkwo as *akwu acha*. In spite of his poor harvest he fed very heavily whenever food was available, and boasted that it would require a strong man to hop over the mound of excrement he deposited in the bush each time he went to 'mourn with the vultures', as he described the call of nature. Once he had a brain-wave and decided to cook and sell food. He bought rice on credit from the Catechist's wife and a gallon of palm wine from the wine tapper (who used to pass daily by the Postal Agency) with the intention of retailing it in bottles at a good profit. After operating for one day, in the shed abandoned for years by Oji, he wound up the hotel business. Before he knew what was happening, the greater part of the rice and the palm wine had passed through his own keen gullet. He had not been able to complete the payment for the rice before his death.

Even though his death was something of a relief to many at Ezinkwo, yet death was death. A member of the community had died and all the other members shared the grief. As Nwankwo had neither the money nor the property to marry, he died without issue. Before long his compound would be overgrown with grass, and his house left to crumble. That was the unhappy fate of the man without male issue, one of the greatest misfortunes that could befall anyone.

Nwankwo's only brother, Okeke, had come to Nwankwo's house to receive sympathisers. Although he had disagreed very violently with Nwankwo because of his laziness, he was now required by custom to give Nwankwo all the funeral rites due to him, in spite of the fact that the deceased had left neither money nor property to help defray these expenses.

'Welcome, Amadi.' Okeke offered his hand as Amadi came to where he sat on a wooden chair. 'When did you come home?'

'Only last night.'

'Oh yes, your father told me you would be returning yesterday. Are there any of our people living in that town?'

'No.'

'Then there is no one to enquire about. How are the people with whom you are studying?'

'They are all well.'

There was a pause. Okeke went into a room, and shortly afterwards emerged with a piece of kolanut on a carved wooden bowl.

'I am sorry this is all that is left in the house,' he apologised as he threw half of the piece of kolanut into his mouth and offered the remaining half to Amadi. Amadi touched the kolanut with the fingers of his right hand, and passed the bowl back, saying he did not eat kolanuts.

'You people and books,' remarked Okeke, for want of

39

something better to say. It was a way of asking about Amadi's studies.

'We are managing.'

Okeke knew why Amadi had come to see him, but it was not proper for him to introduce the topic. He picked up the wooden bowl and tried to focus his attention on it, to give Amadi the chance to state the purpose of his visit. Amadi was aware that the longer the silence the more difficult it would be to break it. He pulled himself together.

'Mazi,' he addressed Okeke, 'this kind of thing I heard on my return yesterday!'

'Well,' replied Okeke, with his eyes on the ground, 'that's what I am seeing. The world is a difficult place.'

'Did they say he died of an injection?'

'Yes.'

'Has anybody discovered who administered the injection?'

'Well, it was this man Oji. Everybody at Ezinkwo knows that.'

Oji was a carpenter. He had worked as an apprentice to the Chairman of the Improvement League but before he had mastered the tricks of the trade he decided to set up on his own. After two years of suffering and poverty he sold his scanty tools and disappeared from the village like a hibernating hawk. Two years later, he returned to Ezinkwo, no longer as a carpenter but equipped with a syringe, tubes of medicines and tablets.

'One thing I can't understand is why our people allow such people without any qualification to give them injections.'

Okeke put a pinch of tobacco into each nostril and offered the box to Amadi who declined politely.

'What else can we do?' he asked. 'Those doctors who come here from time to time give exactly the same injections and charge what no one can pay. My brother was simply unfortunate. He is not the first person in Ezinkwo to receive an injection from Oji.'

'Where is Oji now?'

'Nobody knows. Nobody has seen him since Nwankwo died.'

'Why don't you report him to the police? This kind of thing cannot be allowed to continue.'

Okeke did not see the point. His brother was dead. Reporting Oji might lead to Oji's death too—meaning two deaths in Ezinkwo instead of one. That is, if the police would listen to a poor man like him without demanding all his money. Moreover, the Chairman and the Secretary of the Improvement League had advised him not to report the matter to the police. It would bring no credit to the town. And if Oji had killed someone, his *chi* would reward him appropriately. He who destroys life does not get away with his head. Blood is stronger than many people think.

'*Ndo!*'

'Oh,' replied Okeke. 'The human corpse is not a new thing to the soil. *Obasi-on-high* has done his will.'

As Amadi was still a student he knew Okeke would not expect any money from him. He brushed the seat of his trousers with his hand and moved off to the next house of mourning.

6

At three o'clock the following morning there was a gentle knock on the door of the one-bedroom mud house which Mazi Onuzulike Chukwuka had built for his son so that he could read his books without disturbance. Amadi did not move; his eyes and ears were wide open and his pulse was quickening. The knock was repeated. He flashed his torch and shouted in Ibo: 'Who's that?'

'It's me,' was the gentle reply.

'Is it papa?' he asked, to make quite certain it was his father's voice that he heard.

'Yes.'

Amadi let his father in, wondering what coud be the cause

of such a midnight visit. His mind ran very quickly through the events of the past year, but he could not imagine what he had done to call for such a surprise visit. His father bolted the door, threw his heavy woven cloth over his left shoulder, sat on the only chair in the room and asked Amadi to sit down. When he realised that the visit was not to be a brief one, Amadi struck a match and lit his hurricane lamp. Still puzzled, he sat on his bed.

'My son,' his father began, looking at the floor. 'I am sorry to wake you up at this hour. But you are my first son, and if the ideas of the white man had not carried you away from home, this is the time of night I would call on you whenever we have an important point to discuss. Not only are we free from visitors, but we are also free from the women.'

Amadi still had no clue.

'Since you came home, we have not had the time to talk together. You have been having many visitors, and I thought I should let you have some rest first. You have come from a far place, and, like the lizard that fell from the top of the iroko tree without hurting itself, you deserve praise. There was a time when we thought Arochukwu was the end of the world, and it took us some native weeks to walk from Ezinkwo to Arochukwu, stopping at Ozuakoli to buy cloth which slaves carried for us. Now you go to the University by motor in one day, and I hear the aeroplane can reach the land of the white man in one day. The white man is a spirit you know.'

'Hm . . .,' Amadi grunted. 'Papa, the white man is not a spirit. He has studied what people call science.'

'What is that?'

'I do not know how to explain it. But there are people who study it at the University.'

'True?' His father looked him straight in the face. 'I don't believe the black man can study the thing well, whatever it may be. The day when the black man was a spirit is past. The white man has swept everything away. Think of Mazi Okoro. I remember one day when I had not begun to tie cloth round my waist. The District Officer came to Ezinkwo from Amagu. He wanted Okoro to report at Ndikpa, a town that took a day's walk to reach if you left by the first cock crow. Okoro begged the D.O. to take him in his Morris car, and nearly received a slap for the insolent request. What happened? When the D.O. reached Ndikpa he was surprised to find Okoro waiting for him at the appointed place. The missionaries converted Okoro and made him a lay reader before he died. That was the end of his mysterious powers.'

'Papa, you believe he had mysterious powers and you are yourself a Christian?'

'Er . . .' His father usually stammered if he felt an argument might go against him. 'Yes, I am a Christian, yet there are still many things that puzzle me, and the Catechist has not been able to explain them to us. He asks us not to believe them because they are not in the Bible. Think of the story of Ijoma. The oracle had asked him to roast a yam in the fire, slice it and put oil and pepper inside it, in the way we prepared roast yam for you when you went to school at Obinikpa. He did this, and hid the yam between the bamboo rafters of the roof of his *obi*. He was told that one day, while his hair was being shaved, the razor would strike at something hard. As soon as this happened he should examine the roast yam in the roof and, if anything had happened to it, he would know that death was knocking at his door. The roast yam was hidden away as directed, and for many years nothing happened. Ijoma forgot all about it.

'Then one day, as he was preparing to go to war with his father, a slave shaving his hair struck something hard and shouted that the end of a big nail was sticking from his master's head. Ijoma knew his *chi* was calling him. He rose from the mud bed where he sat, and with trembling hands searched for the roast yam. A tender shoot had sprung from the yam.'

'That's wonderful.'

A cock crew.

Amadi, my son, I must leave you to sleep. What I have come to tell you is that you must wash your eyes in water. It is true the Church has killed many bad things, but the power of the devil is still strong. Many people have been coming to greet you since you returned. Many tell you they

43

are happy that a son of the village is now in the University. But not up to half of them are happy. Many of them laugh with their teeth only, while their hearts are like stone. The only house where you can eat and drink is in Papa Nwakaego's house; perhaps also in Jeremiah's house. Why do you think Nwankwo Nwafor died? He had a long throat which he could not control, and they put " small cough " in a cup of wine which he drank at somebody's second burial.'

' But I heard it was an injection that killed him,' argued Amadi.

' Which injection? It is true Oji has been using one needle for every injection since he returned, but Nwankwo is not the first person to receive an injection from him. The " small cough " had already eaten through his heart and the injection proved too powerful for him, even though Oji's injections are not usually powerful.'

' I hope you have stopped having these injections? '

' Er . . ., yes, . . . no. But what do you expect us to do? The hospital is too far from here, and even if we get there, how are we sure they won't inject ordinary water into us, especially as we do not know anybody working there? Anyway, leave us alone. Our fathers did not visit any hospital and yet they lived to see their grandchildren. What I am telling you is that you must not eat kola or drink palm wine in anybody's house except the people I tell you. As for Nduka, you must be very careful with him. He is a very wicked man. Thanks to God, you do not like women. He can't trap you with his daughters. That's all I want to tell you at present. May day break! '

Amadi bolted the door behind his father, blew out the hurricane lamp and lay down. This was one aspect of his stay at Ezinkwo which never brought him happiness, this idea that everybody was after his blood because he was a brilliant boy. The thought that every other father warned his own son in the same manner was no consolation to him. He had not been allowed to join the Masquerade Society, ostensibly because the Church denounced the Society, but really because it exposed him to the machinations of the wicked. Any time he drank palm wine in his father's house

44

he did so inside a room, lest one of the people he had told that he did not taste palm wine caught him drinking in broad daylight. One thing baffled him. His father, who always warned him to refuse this and that, ate kola and drank palm wine freely in the very houses which he branded as wicked. Could it be that his own father also possessed those mysterious powers which he said the white man had suppressed? He dismissed the thought. His father was illiterate, but he was a Christian, and he could not remember ever seeing any juju hanging from the roof or on the wall anywhere in their compound. Everywhere at Ezinkwo, kolanuts were broken and palm wine was freely passed round. Yet the people lived. Was it only the young who were capable of being poisoned?

'Thanks to God, you do not like women . . .' Could his father really have meant what he said? Amadi remembered the embarrassing episode during his penultimate year in the Secondary School. His father had returned from the farm at 6.30 one evening and saw a girl in Amadi's room. His response to Amadi's 'Good evening, Sir' showed Amadi that he was in for trouble. Shortly afterwards Amadi's mother was summoned to the *obi*. On her way back, she walked into Amadi's room and asked Amadi where his hurricane lamp was, so that she could have it lit. She spoke about the changing season and the rapid approach of darkness and left with the lantern. Miss Morah took the hint and stood up to go. Amadi saw her off, even though this meant passing by his father's *obi*. A long sermon followed the visit. What would people say if they saw a female teacher leaving Amadi's house, or walking side by side with him after dark?

7

When Amadi finally woke up the next morning he felt he had slept for days on end, even though his eyes could not have been closed for more than an hour and a half. He had had a wonderful time with Aduke. Not only had he been able to demonstrate that he was adept at peeling pawpaw but he had also been allowed to eat it. And how relieved he felt at the end of the meal!

When he opened his eyes to discover that he had been dreaming, he was very angry and disappointed, more so when he discovered a huge patch on his pyjamas.

After the gin incident at the University he had begun to feel that Aduke had begun to take a positive interest in him. It was very unusual for a girl—even a female undergraduate for that matter—to identify herself so openly with a boy, especially a boy who had not proposed marriage to her. She must have been aware that by accompanying him to his Hall in the small hours of the morning, she was putting herself at the mercy of the *Crocodile* cartoonist. And yet she had followed him up to the Porter's Lodge and had handed him over to a male student to take him up to his room.

He had gone to Chima to announce his conquest.

'Don't tell me anything about that rude idiot,' said Chima, as he parted his hair in preparation for a trip to the School of Nursing. 'She was making a mistake if she thought I was coming to ask her for a dance.'

'But weren't you?'

'Me!' Chima smacked his chest. 'Imagine the cheek! Ask a first year student for a dance! I might as well eat an ant!'

' I suppose girls from the School of Nursing have a higher status? ' Amadi was not prepared to spare him.

' You may say what you like. The School of Nursing girls are young and fresh. Who wants these academic women? In any case I'm not the man for excuse-me-dances. It's only backboneless men who look forward to excuse-me-dances.' He had his own back on Amadi, who cut him short, and told him the story of his success at the dance. He modified the story to suit himself, claiming that he had pretended to be drunk and his trick had worked marvellously.

' Look here, Mr Chukwuka,' Chima began, showing Amadi the way to the door, ' it seems you can't listen to solid advice. You know the song about University women. Fear those women, they are very clever. If I wake up in the morning and a fowl pursues me, I will run for dear life because I do not know whether the fowl developed teeth overnight. You are too inexperienced to get entangled with a University woman, especially when she is Yoruba.'

Amadi had left Chima with the feeling he always had after a discussion with Chima—the feeling that Chima was not objective. Had he succeeded in keeping away from the End-of-year Dance, he might have taken it that Providence disapproved of his friendship with Aduke. His decision to attend the dance and the events that followed were clearly the work of Providence. More than ever before, he was within sight of his goal and he wanted to follow things up before she lost interest. One voice warned him that he must not make Aduke think he was taking undue advantage of her little show of kindness. He must not behave like the leper who, offered a handshake, is not satisfied with the marvellous gesture, and asks for a full embrace. Time was against him as it was only two days to the end of term.

After leaving Chima he returned to his room, picked up *Things Fall Apart* and went off to Oliaku Hall. He would tell her that he had brought her the novel she had begun to read in his room the previous day, in case she wished to finish it. That would be a good take off; the follow through had been worked out long ago.

Aduke was not in; she had gone off in a green Opel

Kapitan which had called for her at four that afternoon. Amadi looked at his *pronto* watch. Had he come to the Hall direct instead of paying that fruitless visit to Chima he might have caught her before she left. He scribbled a note, telling her why he had come and giving her his holiday address 'in case you may like to know my whereabouts'. He slipped the note into the novel and asked the porter on duty to hand it to her as soon as she returned to the Hall. That was the end of his failure-proof plans for conquering Aduke, for convincing himself that he could conquer a girl without parental influence. Providence was once more against him. This time he decided he was through with the venture.

He pulled off his pyjamas, hung them up meaning to wash them when he went to have his morning bath, and put on his covering cloth. A thought struck him. Why not write to Aduke, telling her of the dream? That might prove to her the depth of his feeling for her. If he wrote the letter quickly he could send it to the Postal Agency in time to catch the mail runner who carried the mails to Eziokwe, the nearest post office. Within 30 minutes the letter was ready. He went to the kitchen to look for his mother.

'Good morning, Ma.'

'Morny, my son,' his mother replied smiling. 'Have you come out from sleep?'

'Yes, Ma.'

'I hope the mosquitoes let you sleep? I always tell these children to shut all doors and windows as soon as darkness approaches, but talking to them is like talking to a blacksmith at work.'

'The mosquitoes did not disturb my sleep. By the way, is it possible to find an envelope for me?'

'Are you writing already? Chiebonam! Go and look in your father's skin bag and see whether you can find an 'nflop there.'

Amadi returned to his room, sealed the letter (written on three sheets of blue writing pad) and affixed a threepenny stamp. He then ran into a most unexpected difficulty. He did not know Aduke's vacation address.

Amadi!' called his mother. 'Write that thing you are writing quickly and get ready. You know it is today that Nwakaego's people are coming to say welcome to you.'

'Oh!' grunted Amadi. He flung the unaddressed envelope on the ground and fell like an understuffed pillow on his bed. 'You have been caught red-handed,' a voice inside him told him unsympathetically. 'I have always warned you that no man aware of the hazards of blindness rushes into things with his eyes wide open. I have warned you that no sensible man carrying a whole elephant on his head joins in hunting crickets. You have now been caught. But it's not too late to mend. That is, if you are prepared to mend your ways. That letter to Aduke does not show that you are.'

He shut his eyes tight, but he could not think. He picked up the unaddressed letter, looked at it for some seconds and tore it to shreds. He wrapped his towel round his neck, dumped his soiled pyjamas into a bucket in his room and announced that he was going to the stream to have a bath.

His mother would not let him walk the distance to the stream. 'Chiebonam!' she shouted, 'why haven't you put water for bath for Amadi?'

'No need to worry, Mama,' pleaded Amadi. 'You know I haven't been to the stream since I returned, and I want to see the old place again. Also, I have some washing to do. I won't stay long.'

It was a bright morning, and the sun had risen early. Amadi's father, who usually left for the farm before Amadi woke up each morning, had already gone, leaving instructions that his breakfast need not be brought to him at the farm as he would be back earlier than usual to receive Nwakaego's people.

The road to the stream had not changed very much since Amadi left Ezinkwo. If anything, the footpath had grown narrower; the owners of the farm plots on both sides of the road, in an attempt to prevent the road from encroaching on their farms, had continued to acquire a bit of the road each planting season. The road meandered between the farms like the Odo river. That it was a good year for yams,

4

was evident from the luxuriant growth on both sides of the road. Some tender and untended yam tendrils brushed his arm as he walked past. The cobs of maize were very tempting, though they needed a little longer to mature.

After walking for about half a mile he emerged on the main road which crossed the town. That was the point where, in his younger days, they had waited for lorries travelling to Onitsha. The oil bean trees they used to climb were still there. His parents had warned him not to climb trees for fear that he might fall and break a bone, but he had always climbed the oil bean trees on that road because their branches were low. Before he learnt to run and leap in order to grasp the lower branches with both hands, he used to take a lift by sitting on Joshua's broad shoulders. Joshua was now in the army; he had become such a bully that everybody had thought the army was the place for him, except his mother who wept bitterly the day he left home, grieved at the thought that ' the mother who has a soldier as a son is childless.'

Since the establishment of the Postal Agency and the growth of a market around it, the road junction had ceased to play the role of a motor station. Everybody now went up to the Postal Agency, or to the Post, as it was abbreviated, to board lorries travelling to Onitsha, and this was where passengers arriving at Ezinkwo were dropped too. The little hut at the old road junction where palm nuts and kernels were at one time sold was dilapidated—everyone had moved up to the Post.

Amadi turned round to look at the narrow snake-like path that led to his father's compound. ' In two years' time, when I get my degree, this will be a motor road.' He fancied himself driving up the gradual slope to their house. ' What a big change it will be from the wooden " cars " my father helped me to build when I still ran about naked! '

The other half of the road to the stream was wider but steeper. It was badly eroded and you had to be very careful going down it. It was very slippery during the rains, and it was said that a pot was broken on it every day the rain fell. As soon as the rains came, few people took pots to the stream; instead they carried buckets or kerosene tins or enamel basins, as they could always pick these up if they fell and return to the stream for a fresh supply. The stream had been given the name *Ike Kute*, as only the strong could return from it with water.

Amadi was the only person that morning in the stream. As he washed the pyjamas, his mind wandered back to Aduke. He decided to wash her too out of his thoughts. Before removing his covering cloth to have a bath, he held the pyjamas at eye level to make sure there was no trace left of Aduke.

8

The compound belonging to Amadi's father was quite large. It was walled round with mud, the top of which was covered with a special type of dry grass which was renewed as soon as it showed signs of decay. Part of the back wall had fallen in, and the fallen mud was temporarily replaced by a fence. There was one entrance into the compound—a gate let in to the front wall and which at night was bolted from the inside for privacy. There were three houses inside the compound. The house that met the eye, as soon as a visitor passed through the front gate, was his father's *obi*. Like the other houses it had a mat roof and mud walls decorated very artistically with geometric patterns. His father's house was the biggest of the three. It had a large space in front—a kind of sitting room. It also had a parlour and two other rooms, in one of which his father slept, leaving the parlour empty except for a few old and abandoned clothes hanging from nails on the walls; the remaining room was used as a store. In his childhood, Amadi had slept in that room with his mother, but now she had a house of her own which she shared with the younger children. She too had a kind of sitting room where she received her own visitors, usually women. The kitchen was behind her house. The third house belonged to Amadi, who enjoyed the privilege of being a first son, and the most educated person at Ezinkwo. It was a single-room house, with a large curtain separating the bed from the rest of the room; he received his guests in the space in front of the curtain.

The only other building in the compound was the latrine. Amadi's father, the Catechist, and the Chairman of the Improvement League were the first at Ezinkwo to dig latrines in their compounds. The latrine was sited near the back wall, and was adjacent to his father's large yam barn.

Amadi heard the characteristic laughter of Nwakaego's father when he was still a quarter of a mile away from the compound—Nwakaego's family must have arrived. He tried to dodge the group by entering the compound through the fence but failed to squeeze his thin body through. He had no option but to pass through the front gate, within sight of everybody.

As soon as the gate swung open every eye turned in his direction.

'He has returned.'

'Welcome!'

'Come and shake hands with us.'

Amadi greeted them all, and asked to be allowed to deposit what he was carrying in the backyard before returning to greet them more fully.

Nwakaego was not in the group. She had been admitted to a Secondary Modern School in January of that year and would not be returning for the holiday till sometime in August. The group was made up of her father, mother, an uncle and a stalwart young man who helped to carry the two-gallon pot of special palm wine, tapped from the oil palm tree and usually described as 'up wine' to differentiate it from the cheaper and more watery palm wine tapped from the raffia palm.

When he returned to the group Amadi was wearing an open shirt and a pair of dark grey Terylene trousers. He shook hands with each person in turn. Nwakaego's mother pulled his arm, sized him up and asked him whether he would ever grow fat.

'Have you been given any kola?' Amadi asked.

'Yes,' they replied, almost in unison. 'Our female in-law has given us enough kola for a meal. It's our male in-law that we are waiting for.'

'Has anyone gone to call him?' asked Amadi, rising as if to go in quest of his father.

'Oh yes,' Nwakaego's father replied. 'Our female in-law has sent Chiebonam to the farm to call him. To drag your father from his farm is as difficult as dragging a child away from its mother's breasts.'

The front door opened and Mazi Onuzulike Chukwuka walked in.

'Husband of yams, welcome!'

'The only farmer who has planted more yams than guinea-fowls can eat, welcome!'

These were the customary titles given to Amadi's father, and he cheerfully accepted them. He loved his yams, and spared no energy to ensure that they were well looked after. He was regarded as the most successful farmer at Ezinkwo and Ezinkwo women paid tribute to him in one of their dances, called the dance of the torch:

He who plants the yams that beat the guinea-fowls
will one day build a double-storeyed house.

Having cheerfully acknowledged the greetings of his prospective in-laws, Mazi Onuzulike asked:

'Have you waited for long?'

'A little, in-law,' replied Nathaniel Ikwuaju, Nwakaego's father, popularly known as Nati. 'I know this is not the best time to meet you at home, but almost every evening for the next week will be taken up by one thing or the other, and people who coin proverbs say that "another time another time is the other name for laziness".'

'You have done well to come at this time,' Mazi Onuzulike went on. 'Even the most conscientious labourer occasionally lays down his shovel to snuff tobacco.' He then turned to Amadi. 'Ask your mother to bring kolanuts while I go in to remove my working clothes.'

53

Nati and his wife said they had already eaten kolanuts.

'If you have eaten, I have not eaten,' insisted Mazi Onuzulike. 'Moreover, kolanuts do not fill the stomach. It is not every day that I and my in-laws break kolanuts together.'

'You have won,' chanted Nwakaego's parents.

Three large kolanuts were lying on a saucer by the time Amadi's father returned to the group. He was dressed in a thick collarless shirt with rolled sleeves, and a brightly-coloured check covering cloth, known at Ezinkwo as *Jioji*. The dominant colours of the cloth were yellow and red.

He lifted the saucer in the direction of Nwakaego's uncle, announcing at the same time: 'In-law, kola has come.'

Nwakaego's uncle responded: 'He who brings kola brings life.'

Mazi Onuzulike repeated the same thing with Nati, asking him to break them.

'The king's kola is in the king's hands,' Nati replied. There was no need to show kola to women at Ezinkwo.

Mazi Onuzulike selected two large kolanuts and asked the stalwart man to put them in the bag for Nati and his brother. 'When the kolanut reaches home it will say from where it has come.'

Amadi was asked to break the kolanut, as was the custom at Ezinkwo, he being the youngest man present. He was handling the kolanut clumsily when Nwakaego's uncle intervened.

'Okeke,' he called on the stalwart young man, 'take the kolanut from him. They don't break kolanuts in the University.'

Okeke was rising to obey the instructions when Amadi's father asked him to warm his seat. 'I don't train my children in that way. This is Ezinkwo, and nobody has said that people who go to University should forget the customs of their people.'

Amadi always felt embarrassed when his father tried to show in public what a disciplinarian he was. He tried to hold on to the smile on his face until it turned into a grimace. After splitting the kolanut into its natural lobes, he handed

54

the saucer to his father. His father asked him to take the saucer to Nwakaego's uncle who took two lobes, broke a piece from one, gave it to Nati and gave the remaining piece to Okeke, he shared the second lobe with Nati's wife. Mazi Onuzulike took one lobe, broke it in two and offered one piece to Amadi who declined, saying he did not eat kola. The fourth lobe was left in the saucer in case any visitor came.

There was a brief silence, during which it became evident that Mazi Onuzulike expected Nati to state the purpose of their visit, even though the purpose was already known. Nati took the hint, cleared his throat and sat up.

' My in-law, there is no need for a long speech.' He pulled his fingers, moving from the fingers of the left hand to those of the right, and making each finger crack in turn. ' You know why we have come . . . It is simply to say welcome to our son, and to thank God for looking after him well during the past year, and for bringing him safely back from such a long distance. That is all. We can't say we have brought him anything.' He turned towards the stalwart young man. ' Okeke, bring that pot.'

Okeke heaved the two-gallon pot of ' up wine ' into the middle of the room.

' Mama Ego '—that was how Nati addressed his wife—' have you anything to say? '

Nwakaego's mother rose from her seat, went towards the front wall and returned with a long market basket she had left on top of the wooden pegs which were knocked into the wall at regular intervals. She emptied the contents of the basket on the floor of the *obi*: two well fed and noisy cocks, four large yams and two big dried fish, each shaped like the letter O by the fisherman who had dried it.

' Mazi, our in-law,' she remained, standing, ' this should not be called anything. If it were the time for our son Amadi had not entered the University, we would have cooked food for him in our house. Now that he is there how can I cook for him? Have I been there, or did I ever have any training anywhere? To make matters worse my daughter, Nwakaego, has not yet returned from her College, so we thought the best

55

thing is to bring these few things to Amadi our son. Let him do what he likes with them.'

'Amadi rose and thanked them: 'Thank Sir! Thank Ma!', and shook hands with them.

'Amadi, call your mother to see what our eyes are seeing,' instructed Mazi Onuzulike.

His parents were very appreciative. 'In-laws, you have sealed our lips with your kindness. We trust that God will pay you back more than double what you have spent on us today. All we ask is long life. Everything will turn out well. Was it not the bed bug who asked its children to be patient because what is hot will eventually be cold?'

Nwakaego's uncle spoke next. 'In-laws, this is not a time for words. We shall speak when the time for speaking comes. Our connection with your family did not begin today, and it is not ending tomorrow. Forget that today God above has blessed you through your yams and this son. Remember in those days when this my brother was still a child in our mother's arms, with the mucus trickling down his nostrils. Who was that white man in the mission then?'

Amadi's father supplied the answer. 'The white man whose head shone like the full moon.'

'Yes, that's him. Remember how he saw us one day shooting lizards and asked us why we did not come to his school? Remember the advice he gave us to seek the black goat before the approach of darkness? When I tell these children how people suffered in our youth, picking palm nuts and cracking them for sale to get money for school fees, they think I am telling them fairy stories. You remember it was after we had escaped being sold at Ozuakoli by a trader who hired us to carry cloth there for him, that we took the decision which is responsible for our presence here today. I shall stop now, lest I lick my fingers in a hurry. When the time comes for speaking, I shall speak.'

'Welcome,' responded Mazi Onuzulike. 'As we used to say in those days, why hurry to go to Church, is the missionary leaving today? Why lick your fingers in a hurry, are you going to hang them up in the ceiling? Don't worry, by the help of God above, the time to speak is coming.'

Amadi's mother removed the presents to her house, and Amadi went for cups for the palm wine.

'My in-law,' called Nwakaego's uncle, 'please give me a bit of that snuff again. It cleared my head like a broom the other time I snuffed it.'

The snuff box was passed to him. He gave the top a few taps with his finger—to shake the snuff down and so prevent any flying away when he opened the box. He opened it cautiously, took a liberal quantity with the first finger of his right hand, pressed it down with the thumb, dug the finger again into the box and transferred as much snuff as he could collect into one nostril. In the same way he transferred a similar quantity of snuff into the other nostril. He returned the box, cleaned out his fingers, opened his eyes and mouth wide, and sneezed.

'There must be something you drop into your snuff. It goes right into my brain. If I had had snuff like this in those days, I would have gone to England.'

Everyone enjoyed the joke.

When Amadi's mother returned, she was carrying two large plates of a dish known at Ezinkwo as *abacha ncha*—a delicacy prepared from thin dry slices of boiled cassava, mixed with a slippery oil concoction. It was usually eaten with dried fish or crayfish and was believed to be the luxury condiment for palm wine. It was never eaten at Ezinkwo as the main meal; it was prepared either on festive occasions, or as an emergency dish on occasions like this, when the preparation of *foo-foo* and bitterleaf soup would take too much time. Amadi had heard many men say that it was the medicine for excessive drinking; no amount of palm wine could intoxicate them if the foundation for the wine was laid with a plate of *abacha ncha*. Some people did not eat it because they said it usually purged them.

When the first cup of palm wine was passed to each of the women, she went down on her knees, drank some of the wine and gave the rest to her husband, saying 'Thank Sirs'. As there was plenty of wine, their husbands authorised them to drain the cups and to have some more.

Nwakaego did not feature prominently in the discussions

except that her father recounted the difficulty he was having in paying her fees in Modern School. She had lived with Amadi's parents practically all through her primary schooldays and her fees during this time were paid by Amadi's father. Mazi Onuzulike had, however, found it difficult to pay all her fees when she moved to Modern School, for even though Amadi was being sponsored in the University by the Ezinkwo Improvement League he still wrote to his father for money from time to time, and he was not their only child.

In fact Nwakaego's success in the entrance examination to Modern School had caused a small dilemma. Nati considered it a waste to spend all that money on a girl when he had a number of sons in the primary school. What was the point in spending much money on a girl who was already betrothed? As soon as she got married all her education would be wasted when she took her place in the kitchen. Even if she were to gain a certificate that would enable her to work after marriage, her earnings would only flow into her husband's pockets. Nati was convinced that Nwakaego had had sufficient education for her role as a housewife. After all, it was common knowledge that the Catechist's wife who was the most enlightened woman in the village, did not go beyond Class Two Infant at Ugwuogba. Yet she could read and write, and had been seen in conversation with the white Bishop. Did Nwakaego's mother ever hear as much as the ringing of school bells in her youth? And was she not a perfect wife?

The climax came the day Mazi Onuzulike told him that Amadi had written to say he would not marry a girl with only the Standard Six certificate. Nati could not well damn the consequences, remembering how indebted he already was to Mazi Onuzulike—a debt that only the marriage of his daughter to Amadi could wipe out. Both men had approached the Chairman of the Improvement League to know whether the League could help them out. The Chairman looked very sympathetic, especially as Nwakaego was the first daughter of the town to aspire to post-primary education and he promised to try and convince the League.

But the League refused to help. A member recalled that

the first award from the League had gone to Amadi. Must the second go to Nati's daughter who was betrothed to Amadi? Did Mazi Onuzulike Chukwuka pay higher subscriptions than other people? Another member thought, like Nati, that it was a waste of money to train a girl already betrothed. Moreover, the benefit to be derived from training someone in the Secondary Modern School was not very obvious.

A compromise was agreed on whereby Mazi Onuzulike would help Nati to pay the fees. Nati was not very happy about this arrangement but had no alternative but to agree. Even though he was helped by his wife's brother, he took every opportunity to recount his difficulties, and Mazi Onuzulike was not surprised to hear him recount them yet again for Amadi's benefit.

9

Mazi Onuzulike did not allow his son to attend the funeral rites of the late Nwankwo Nwafor. Nwankwo had refused to be converted and had died a heathen. He had gone to church only once in his life, because he heard that a white missionary was to talk to the congregation in Ibo and he did not want to miss the fun. He knew that if he became a Christian he would be called upon to pay all the innumerable church dues and levies. The Mission fund at Ezinkwo at that time was known as ' the bag that was open at both ends '; no matter how many dues and levies were paid there was always an appeal to members for more money. In addition to the monetary collections, each church member was often asked to supply, at his own expense, mats and bamboos for repairing the church building and to help in carrying out the repairs without payment for his labour. Nwankwo felt he was not wealthy enough to be a Christian, and there was no point in enrolling, only to be suspended the next day for failure to pay his dues.

Mazi Onuzulike was a staunch member of the Church and would not indulge in any heathen practice or allow any member of his household to do so. He renounced practices such as the pouring of libations to dead ancestors, and he would not taste any drink, however tantalizing, if part of it had been poured on the floor as a libation. But this did not mean that to him dead members of the family had no further influence on the living members, on the contrary, he believed that his elder brother, who had died the year before Amadi was born, had returned to life for Amadi resembled him in every respect, even in the depth of his voice.

He would not hear of his children being initiated into the Masquerade Society. It was a heathen practice. The fact that he had belonged to the Society in his youth, before his conversion, did not make any difference. He could be heard bragging that none of his sons would be initiated.

Many boys in Amadi's age group had pulled his leg because he did not want to be initiated. Some derisively called him a girl. Some threatened to flog him till he bled (his great learning notwithstanding) if he made the mistake of coming home during the *ikeji* festival.

' What of my father? ' Amadi would ask. ' He has made it clear that he will not allow me to be initiated.'

That made them tease him all the more. ' The only boy who has a father! As if Joshua who wears the *Odo* mask is not the son of a churchwarden! Can't you do what he did? '

' What did he do? ' asked Amadi.

' Go and ask him,' was the reply.

Amadi did and discovered that Joshua had sent money home through the Postal Agent who arranged the initiation. During his first term at the University, he did the same thing. He knew his father would be disappointed if he heard about it, but he felt convinced that his acceptance of Christianity should not prevent him from joining the Masquerade

Society—a society that was purely social in function and which had been in existence before his father was born. All that was demanded of him was a fee of five shillings; because of his special circumstances the Society did not insist on the food and drinks that should have accompanied the money. The Postal Agent undertook to reveal the secrets of the Society to him on his return, as it would have been improper to write them in a letter, lest the letter fell into the hands of a novice or a woman. There was a clear understanding that everything must be kept secret from Amadi's father.

The Postal Agent had not yet found time to disclose the secrets to Amadi. Amadi had, however, known practically every secret, including the members' signal, for many years, but it was indiscreet to show that he possessed this knowledge; the penalty for disclosing publicly the secrets of the Society —unmasking a masquerader, as it was called—was high, and even ended occasionally in loss of life. Everybody in the village knew the fate of the overzealous churchwarden who unmasked a masquerader publicly one Christmas Day many years ago, because the masquerader had chased a woman into the church thus breaking the gentleman's agreement which forbade masqueraders to enter the church building. All his sheep and goats were mercilessly slaughtered in revenge, and were it not for the timely plea of the Chairman of the Improvement League, a much respected member of the society who, in his youth, had carried the huge *mgbedike* mask, he would have received a couple of strokes from the notorious cane that turned men into lepers.

Amadi could not go to Nwankwo Nwafor's funeral because it was a heathen ceremony. Instead his father took him to the second burial ceremony of James, the oldest member of the Church at Ezinkwo, who was known by everybody at Ezinkwo, Christian or not, as *Nna anyi*, meaning 'our father'. He had died in late March. This was a very bad time of the year; it was in the heat of the planting season when food is generally scarce and people are compelled to depend on special famine foods like water yams, boiled and dried coco-yams, corn meals and breadfruit dishes. *Nna anyi* James was not the man to be accorded a scanty second burial so the

61

ceremony was put off till August, a time of plenty, and the month when there is usually a break in the rains. All the dead man's children had come home for the occasion.

The early morning clouds had cleared away, to the joy of everyone. But by eleven in the morning everyone was sure the rain would pour down in bucketfuls, in spite of the fact that it had not rained for the past week. The village rain-maker was reported to be angry because he had not been placated, and when the clouds thickened many suggested that something should be taken to him, especially as his charges were only nominal. *Nna anyi*'s children conferred together, and one of them, a sawyer in Benin Province, said he was off to the rainmaker if the others were afraid to go. Their old mother stopped him, almost at the point of tears.

'What would *Nna anyi* think of us in his grave?' she pleaded. 'You know how he often preached against these rainmakers when he was alive. You remember how angry he was when somebody suggested seeing a rainmaker to ensure that rain did not fall during the last Anniversary cele-brations. I will not live to see you do what will make him talk to us from his grave.'

By two o'clock in the afternoon when the ceremonies were about to begin, the sky was clear to the joy of everyone, but especially to the deceased's wife, the Catechist and Mazi Onuzulike who had all declared that the power of God would always overcome the power of evil. The breeze that blew the rain clouds away had not dropped completely; it was still powerful enough to sway the maize leaves. The sun had appeared, though the breeze minimised its effect. It was a cool wind which was usually regarded as a sign that there would be no rain.

When Amadi and his father arrived at *Nna anyi*'s home, the compound was almost full. A temporary shelter had been constructed out of palm fronds supported by bamboo pillars; it stretched from almost the front wall of the large compound to the back wall. All the benches in the village church had been moved to the compound for the ceremony. They were arranged in rows, in such a way that two rows of guests faced each other, with a long row of benches between them for the food and drinks. Tables and folding chairs broke the monotony of the rows; these were reserved for the village V.I.P.s and the special guests from other towns. Amadi and his father saw these reserved seats when they entered the compound but meandered away from them as it would be considered presumptuous to sit on them without first being invited to do so. They were ushered to them later (though they sat at different tables), Amadi in recognition of his learning, and his father as the principal farmer and a leading member of the Church at Ezinkwo. In the meantime, however, they took their seats on the benches, in a corner from where they could see everyone as they arrived.

In one part of the compound the women were dancing. It was not the traditional Ibo women's dance for the Church had forbidden its women members to take part in these dances which it described as heathen. The women wore their everyday dresses, a covering cloth and blouse, and sang Christian songs composed by themselves. Their instruments were few and simple—a pot with a long neck and a circular hole on one side, called the *udu* and used to provide the beat, a *shekere* made out of a calabash with a network of dark seeds on the outside, and small drums which the women beat with little art. The dancers clapped their hands to the beat as they danced round a circle singing:

> *Whose work are you doing?*
> *I am doing Our Lord's work!*
> *Whose work are you doing?*
> *I am doing Our Lord's work!*
> *When Our Lord will come,*
> *He will carry us in His arms to heaven,*
> *He will wipe away our tears.*

The dancing stopped as a Morris Minor pulled up outside the compound. Children ran out to see who it was, and all eyes turned towards the entrance. The Pastor of Amagu, wearing a white suit and collar, stepped in, followed by a lean white man, also in a clerical collar, who was carrying something under his arm. The Catechist ran to meet them and took them to their table—the most special place of all. Every eye was on the white man who maintained a steady smile. The ceremony began.

The Catechist announced a hymn and read the first verse aloud. A girl gave the lead by singing the first line after which she was joined by everybody. It was a well known song for the dead, expressing the hope that both the dead and those now living would one day meet ' on the other side of the river '. The Catechist read each verse aloud before it was sung, though this was not necessary as the older men and women knew every line of it by heart, having sung it on many similar occasions. An appropriate lesson was read from Revelations, after which the Pastor, the Reverend James Dinkpa, was called upon ' to tell the gathering a few words '.

The Pastor in charge of Amagu Parish, the Reverend J. Dinkpa, had visited Ezinkwo many times in the course of his duties, for Ezinkwo Church was one of the leading Churches in Amagu Parish. He knew the late James, whom he referred to as his namesake, very well. He reminded the people of the story of James's life, how he had risen from the lowly position of a rejected twin—discovered like Moses near the bush—to become the most influential member of the Church at Ezinkwo, nay, in the whole of Amagu Parish.

' As I have told you time and time again,' he preached, ' God does not reject the men who accept him. From the ash in the kitchen he lifts up the beggar. God has blessed the late James in many ways. Look at his compound, how large and attractive! Look at his sons and daughters! An orphan who, till his death, did not know father or mother, brother or sister. When a maize is ripe what happens? It is removed from the farm and stored in a place specially prepared for it. James lived to see his grandchildren, and to see Ezinkwo Church stand on its feet. On the 28th of March God took him away from us, to the better place. Fellow Christians, we have not come here to weep. We have come here today to rejoice that our great Church leader is now with Him who leads us all. May we rise for a short prayer.'

After the prayer the Pastor introduced his white friend. The gathering was excited to see the lean white missionary who had a reputation for destroying the most dreaded shrines.

The white man added to his popularity when later he accompanied the dancing women on the accordion which he had been carrying under his arm when he entered the compound.

The formalities over, it was time to serve the food. A cow had been slaughtered, one of the greatest marks of respect that can be paid to a dead person. The breaking of kola-nuts, mixed with slices of coconuts, was followed by bowls of *abacha ncha*. Then came large bowls of rice, followed by mounds of cassava *foo-foo*. The meat came last and was carried in wide wooden trays which were carved locally. Owing to the disputes that usually arose with the sharing of meat, the Church Committee had ruled that meat should always come last and that it should be cut into equal pieces. The practice of giving certain members larger pieces had caused so much misunderstanding that it had had to be abolished, the Church Committee arguing that every person was equal in the eyes of God. The Pastor and the ' white destroyer of shrines ' were served their own dishes inside a room in the house; later, when they drove away from Ezinkwo in the evening, the Morris Minor sagged with the weight of drinks and presents.

During the noise that accompanied the sharing of the meat and the wine, Amadi noticed a girl approaching the compound. She was wearing a smart blue dress. It was beginning to grow dark and it was not possible for him to make out from where he sat who the girl was. She slowed down as she came near the entrance, paused, and then moved out of his vision, beneath one of the orange trees that stood outside the compound. The undergraduate spirit in him surged up. He lost interest in the meat, excused himself from the table and made for the entrance.

' Nwakaego! ' he shouted as he stood within a few yards of his bride-to-be. His first impulse was to embrace her, but he checked himself.

The girl smiled and turned her eyes in the direction of the orange tree. ' Good evening, Sir.'

' When did you return? ' he asked.

' Just now, Sir.'

' I'm very happy to see you again. I have been expecting you for a long, long time.'

Nwakaego picked up an orange leaf lying on the ground and tore it into tiny bits. Her fingers were pretty.

' Are you very anxious to go in there? ' asked Amadi pointing inside the compound.

Nwakaego replied in Ibo, saying she only wanted to tell her parents that she had returned. They had left a message for her in the house, telling her to look for them in *Nna anyi*'s compound.

Amadi was tempted to carry her straight off to his little hut. She was full of natural charm without being aware of it. She reminded him of a girl in his class at the primary school who was nicknamed ' Natural '. If hawkers of make-ups depended on girls like ' Natural ' they would run out of business; she did not own as much as a tin of the cheapest powder on the local market. Her school uniform was sewn by the local seamstress who also sewed uniforms for most of the girls in the school. Yet each time she appeared for the early morning inspection she looked the showpiece of a master craftsman. Many were angry but nobody was surprised when the polygamous chief of her village, who had a keen eye for ' all things bright and beautiful ', withdrew her from school in Standard Two and added her to his collection of wives.

Nwakaego was very much like ' Natural '. Both of them confirmed Amadi's belief that good looks are sent from above. As the dog said, good teeth are sent from *Chi*; even if men were to spend every hour of their lives cleaning their teeth with chewing sticks or toothbrushes, they would never be as white as the dog's.

As soon as she was recognised inside the compound, her name went round. ' Nwakaego, the daughter of Nati, the girl Mazi Onuzulike is marrying for his son.' Her mother rushed out to embrace her, followed by Amadi's mother and many other women. Before they could leave the compound she had shaken hands with almost everybody present. Each time she was about to move away someone shouted to her: ' Out daughter, come and shake hands with us.' Amadi stood aloof and watched her, feeling very proud of her.

Within that short time he had noticed that she had a long segmented neck, lovely dimples on both cheeks, wonderful legs . . .

His father must have read his thoughts. He disliked public displays, and even though everybody at Ezinkwo knew Nwakaego had been betrothed to Amadi from birth he did not think the time had come when she and Amadi should move about together publicly. He sent a boy to call Amadi, on the pretext that someone wanted to meet him. Amadi could not disobey his father and Mazi Onuzulike kept him by his side till Nwakaego had left the compound with her mother. He sulked on the way home, but his father decided to take no notice of this.

A postal slip for a registered packet was waiting for him as he entered his one-room house. He picked it up, looked at it blankly, and let it drop on his small table. There was no point bothering about a postal slip on a Saturday night, the Postal Agency would not open before Monday.

He went to his mother in the kitchen. 'Mama, you have seen Nwakaego?'

'Yes.'

'I didn't know she had grown so much.'

'Oh yes,' his mother replied. 'Don't you know that College stretches young people? I remember how rapidly you grew when you went into College the first time.'

'And she is so beautiful?' He spoke as if he needed confirmation from his mother. She made no comment.

'I am happy she will soon be my wife.'

'Because she is beautiful?' asked his mother.

'No, Ma, not because of that alone.'

'I would have said that you talk like a child. But aren't you still a child, or is it because you are in the University?'

On Monday morning he told his mother he was going to the Postal Agency to claim his registered postal packet. He had told Nwakaego, when she came to their house after morning service on Sunday, that he would call at her house on his way there so that they might go together. She feared her mother might not allow her to accompany him, and on his

67

suggestion, they agreed to meet at the apple tree half-way to the Postal Agency. When he arrived there she was nowhere to be seen. He discovered he had left the slip in the pocket of the shirt he had meant to wear, before deciding to wear *agbada*, and dashed back to the house. By the time he got back to the tree, Nwakaego was walking towards the Postal Agency. She wore a pink dress, and looked very ravishing from the back. Amadi caught up with her, full of apologies and explanations for his lateness. He tried to hold her by the hand but she quickly swung her hand away, saying in Ibo that it was not proper.

The registered packet was a book, Amadi recognised the sender's writing and refused to tear the packet open.

' Do you know what's inside it? ' Nwakaego asked, as usual in Ibo, although Amadi spoke in English, in an attempt to make her reply in English.

' Oh yes.' He hesitated. ' It's a book on Geomorphology which I sent for from the University Bookshop.'

Nwakaego looked at the packet, as if there was something of interest in it. ' But look at the post-office mark.' She pointed at it. ' It reads Makurdi.'

Amadi thought rapidly. Nwakaego turned the packet round. ' And it says here that the sender is Miss Aduke Olowu, c/o United Missionary College, Makurdi.'

Amadi succeeded in hiding his confusion, largely because Nwakaego was too shy to look him in the face.

' Miss Aduke Olowu? Who can she be? ' he asked. ' These Yoruba names often confuse me. Wait a minute! ' He gave the impression he was thinking, and then burst out laughing, sounding, he thought, very convincing. ' I know who it is. It's my classmate, Idowu Oloke, trying to play a joke on me. I gave him the money for the book just before I left because he said he was spending two months with his brother, who is a Lecturer in Geology at the University, before going to Makurdi to spend the rest of the vacation with his elder sister who is teaching at the United Missionary College there. It's possible that he bought the book just before he left the University and decided to post it to me from Makurdi. His trick almost worked! Bozo! He wanted me to jump for joy thinking I have made a catch, not knowing the beautiful angel I have here.' He pressed Nwakaego to his side and gently took the book from her.

At the apple tree they parted, hoping to meet again in Amadi's house as soon as Nwakaego's mother allowed her to call.

The letter from Aduke was not worth the lies Amadi had been forced to tell. If he had had prior knowledge of the contents he could have opened the packet in front of Nwakaego. There was nothing to hide in a letter as plain as this:

Dear Mr Chukwuka,

I am sending back your copy of Chinua Achebe's *Things Fall Apart*. It is a pity I was away when you brought it for me. It was very kind of you.

I enjoyed the book tremendously. I was struck by the similarity between the ways of life of the Ibos and the Yorubas; many of the incidents described in the novel could have taken place in a Yoruba village. Perhaps we are not as different as we appear to be!

I am doing a vacation job here which is a bit strenuous. I hope you are having an enjoyable vacation.

All the best.

Yours sincerely,

A. Olowu

Amadi hid the letter away in his suitcase. ' Univeristy women,' he murmured, ' so disciplined that they can't let go a careless expression of emotion, even in a personal letter! '

10

Adanma n'mem ofu,
Kwadebekwa n'iga ana!
Ada nma n'imem ofu,
Ewo na omume gi asorom!
Ina'bu so nma,
Ina'bu so nma,
Gbo, agaeli nma eli ?
Ewo, na omume gi asorom!

For more than an hour Amadi rolled on his bed. He could not get out of his head that highlife piece, played by one of the leading Nigerian dance bands. In it, the singer asks his beautiful wife to pack bag and baggage—to pack even the ash in the kitchen, as Ezinkwo people would say; her behaviour left much to be desired and her husband would have her in his house no more. Beauty, he sang, is not edible; good behaviour is a much more important quality in a wife.

This was one of those popular pieces which usually transforms every dancer into a vocalist. When it was played at Chikwelu's party everyone joined in the singing, everyone except Amadi and Nwakaego, Nwakaego because she was sulking and Amadi because anger was weighing him down.

Mr Chikwelu, a young teacher at the Ezinkwo Primary School, had just passed the Higher Elementary Certificate Examination with credits in Arithmetical Processes and an Approved African Language, and he was celebrating with friends. He had attended a Secondary School before proceeding to the Teacher Training College; he was drawn towards Amadi, partly in the hope that Amadi would give him a few tips on how to secure admission to the University, and partly because he longed to learn ballroom dancing and believed that every undergraduate from the University was an accomplished dancer. He had in his possession his elder brother's portable spring gramophone and he managed to persuade Amadi to give organised dancing lessons to himself and five other teachers who also wanted to learn. Amadi taught them all he had learnt of the Quickstep and Waltz. When they pressed him to teach them the Blues, Slow Foxtrot and Tango, all of which he had found too intricate to learn, he told them to master first what he had taught them: ' You do not plunge your fingers right inside hot soup, you begin from the sides of the soup pot and then work gradually inwards.'

Mr Chikwelu knew about Amadi's attachment to Nwakaego and wanted to send a separate invitation to her, but Amadi had told him there was no need as he would bring her along.

It had been an uphill task all the way.

' What will Mama say if she hears I am dancing with men? ' she asked Amadi in Ibo.

' What is wrong with dancing with men? After all don't we have our moonlight dances when men and women play together? How did Sunday come to be called ' the man who lands in the midst of women '? Was it not because of the traces of camwood dye seen on his chest each morning following the moonlight games? '

Nwakaego made no comment.

' Shall I come for you, or shall we meet at the apple tree? '

' I am sure Mama will not agree.'

' You go and tell her first! '

Amadi did not see his fiancée again till the day of the party. A voice told him that something had gone wrong somewhere. Another told him not to bother; at Ezinkwo silence was usually interpreted as acquiescence. An hour before the party he decided to send Chiebonam with a note to Nwakaego, ostensibly to remind her of the time but more to reassure himself that she was coming. He was finding Nwakaego not quite his idea of an ideal companion, and certainly not a girl to take for granted. The feeling he had when Chiebonam returned with a message from her saying that she could not go was one of anger rather than surprise.

He left the house thirty minutes before the time fixed for the party and made for Mazi Nati's house. He saw Nwakaego's mother in a small bush outside their compound, collecting leaves for the goats.

' Good afternoon, Ma.'

' Dafnun, son; have you come out from sleep? '

' Yes, Ma.'

' What of my male in-law? '

' He is well.'

' And my female in-law? '

' She is well. Is Nwakaego in? '

' I think so. Nwa-k'e-go! ' she called.

' Ma! '

' I have come to take her out.' 'Amadi was serious. He fixed his eyes on his future mother-in-law, almost like a cock on the offensive.

' To which place? ' Nwakaego's mother was once more cutting tender leaves for the goats, and Amadi's looks were lost on her. She spoke without looking at him.

' To the school,' Amadi replied.

' What for? '

' She knows.'

' She will not go with you.'

' Why not? '

Nwakaego's mother now stood to her full height, about 5 foot 3 inches. Amadi could read from the expression on her face that what she was about to say might be unpleasant.

' Because I do not want her to go. My daughter is not going to sell herself to those male teachers. When you marry her you can do what you like with her. Now she is my daughter, and I say she is not going anywhere.'

For a brief while Amadi was not certain what to do. He bit his lower lip and turned away from his mother-in-law-to-be to see whether he could think what line he should take. He looked at his wrist watch and found he still had a quarter of an hour to spare. Uppermost in his mind was the feeling that he must stand on his dignity. He saw nothing unreasonable in his demand and was not prepared to concede even an inch of ground. ' My stand now will determine to a considerable extent the kind of control I shall have over Nwakaego when she becomes my wife. Is this the kind of understanding mother-in-law I am to expect? A bird that gives off twenty droppings while still in the air, how many will it give off when it lands on its two feet? '

How could he explain matters to Mr Chikwelu? He disliked washing his inner clothes in the open stream; moreover Mr Chikwelu had specially invited Nwakaego in order to swell the number of girls at the party, and he would be disappointed if she did not accompany him.

He was still standing outside the entrance to the compound when Nwakaego's mother, who was now placing the leaves within reach of the goats' mouths, spoke to him: ' My man, why do you remain standing there? Do you want to draw visitors to our house? '

' I am coming, Ma.'

' If you want to sit down, we have a chair for you.'

' This place where I am is all right for me.'

' It is all right,' agreed Nwakaego's mother as she picked up her matchet and went towards the enclosure behind the kitchen for a much needed bath. ' Who ever tells a grown up man to come out of the sun? '

Amadi entered the compound, making his way slowly towards Nwakaego's mother's house. Nwakaego who had followed the proceedings from her room came out as soon as she heard the sound of the water on her mother's body.

' Good afternoon, Sir,' she whispered, her eyes on the ground.

' What's all this about? ' Amadi had no time for salutation. He needed every effort to keep his voice down.

Nwakaego was looking at the patterns she was forming on the sand with her right toe. ' Mama is angry that you did not obtain permission from her before asking me to go out with you. Moreover she is afraid of the stories that will soon spread that I dance with men in public . . .'

' Nwakaego, what are you doing there? ' That was her mother. Amadi knew when the splashing of the water stopped abruptly that his mother-in-law was spreading her

73

ears wide open to catch one or two words. He knew she would be disappointed because Nwakaego talked in low tones and the wind was not blowing in her mother's direction. Nwakaego promptly returned to her room.

'Mama, I am sorry if I have offended you,' began Amadi It was his turn this time to draw patterns on the ground with the point of his shoe.

'Who says you have offended me?'

'I know I have.'

'In what way?'

'By not telling you that I want to go up to the school with Nwakaego.'

'Did I complain about that?'

'No,' replied Amadi. 'But I know I should have told you first.'

She paused for a while. 'My son, I can't blame you very much. You are still a small boy, even though it is true that you are in the University and know more book than any-one else at Ezinkwo. This thing you are going to, what is it?'

Amadi explained the purpose of the party, cutting out everything to do with dancing.

'Didn't I hear you are going there to dance?'

'Who said so?' asked Amadi evasively.

'I should have said! I don't want to train my daughter in that way. Nwakaego, do you want to go with him?'

'Yes, Ma.'

'All right, you must see that you come back in time, and that you return direct. I don't want to hear that you visited any other place.'

It has been a hard won fight, though Amadi as he walked to the school with his fiancée.

'Good afternoon, Mr Chukwuka, I am glad you could come after all. We haven't been able to start because we were waiting for you. I feel you should grace the occasion by taking the chair.'

'Good afternoon, Mr Chikwelu,' Amadi replied. 'I am very sorry that we are unavoidably late. A stranger from a distant place came to see my father just as we were about to

74

set out for this place. There was no one in the house, so we were compelled to take him to the farm where Papa was working, over a mile away. And, as you know, it is impossible for one person to be cooking food and at the same time tapping palm wine.'

Nwakaego suppressed a giggle. Amadi and Mr Chikwelu turned in her direction. ' By the way, I don't think you have met my fiancée, Miss Nwakaego Ikwuaju. Nwakaego, here you meet Mr Chikwelu, one of our senior teachers and a good friend of mine.'

' Pleased to meet you, Miss Ikwuaju.' Mr Chikwelu put out his right hand for a handshake. Nwakaego took the outstretched hand with her two palms and curtsied, without saying anything.

' There are chairs for both of you on the platform. We'll start as soon as you take your seats.' Mr Chikwelu rushed into the store he was using as a temporary pantry to make sure that all was in order.

' Who is going to sit up there? ' asked Nwakaego disapprovingly.

' It's specially for you and me. I am the Chairman for the occasion.'

' I don't want to sit there,' she replied, attempting a half spin on her right heel.

' Why not? ' asked Amadi, surprised at his own coolness.

' How can I sit there, with everybody staring at me? '

' Come on, my friend,' and Amadi took her by the left hand and led her to the platform. ' You can't come here to disgrace me. Many other girls would be happy to have the opportunity which you are carelessly throwing away.'

The party started off well. One of the teachers made an elaborate introduction : ' Amadi Chukwuka Esquire, without equivocation the most learned personality in this august assembly . . .' Amadi proved equal to the occasion. He had suspected he might be called upon to take the chair and before leaving the house he had rehearsed his opening remarks.

' Ladies and Gentlemen,' he began. ' After hearing all the encomiums lavished on me by the last speaker, I am sure you are expecting more than I am capable of giving you this afternoon, especially as it was only a minute ago that Mr Chikwelu asked me to take the chair without showing me the programme. As we say at Ezinkwo, even the strong man can be beaten by a surprise visit. I hope therefore that you will pardon me if I fall short of what you have been led to expect . . .'

In spite of his apparent unpreparedness, he reproduced his well rehearsed speech extremely well and from time to time received tremendous ovations.

All the speeches were packed into the first half of the programme. The toasts followed the traditional breaking of kolanuts: the toast to Mr Chikwelu and the response, the toast to the guests and the response, goodwill speeches by the Headmaster of the school and four other people, including a female teacher who spoke for the women. Biscuits, sandwiches and drinks, palm wine, kola and beer were still passing round freely when Mr Chikwelu announced that the floor was open for dancing. The first record had no luck; nobody was bold enough to take the floor.

Mr Chikwelu walked up to Amadi and whispered into his ear: 'Nobody will dance unless you give the lead.'

'Is that so? O.K.; play a good highlife, and make sure you join me with one of those lady teachers as soon as I set the ball rolling.'

As Mr Chikwelu tiptoed to the gramophone, Amadi asked Nwakaego to get ready for a dance.

'What did you tell Mama?' she asked.

'Forget about that. Your mother is not here, unless you go home to tell her which I know you will not do. Moreover, she only objected to your dancing with the teachers, not with the man who is going to marry you.'

'But I have told you that I can't dance.'

'You can. It's highlife, which is no different from the samba every child at Ezinkwo dances. Moreover, it's with me that you are dancing.' The music had begun.

> *Adanma, you have ruined me,*
> *You must go back home*

Adanma, you have ruined me,
Your conduct is appalling.

Nwakaego danced well, and was loudly applauded when she negotiated a beautiful spin on her left foot. Chikwelu obeyed Amadi to the letter, he took a lady teacher, taller than he was and very slim, and without waiting to warm up, began dancing the *amakekwu* style for which he was well known. He soon drew attention away from Amadi and Nwakaego. Others joined in, till all the ladies were dancing.

' What's the matter? ' asked a bewildered Amadi as Nwakaego suddenly broke away from him.

' Papa,' she whispered in reply.

' What about Papa? I thought it was Mama a short while ago.'

' Can't you see him coming up the hill? ' She moved towards the wall.

' Nwakaego, I just cannot understand all this. If it's a crime for your father to catch you dancing with me, you'd better sit down there and dance with the chair! '

Amadi walked up to the platform, took a long but unseeing look at the programme and tried to collect himself. He came down again and posted himself beside Nwakaego. The music was still on:

You may be pretty,
You may be pretty,
But who eats beauty ?
Your conduct is appalling.

How true, thought Amadi. Beauty was inedible; behaviour was much more important. The dancers all seemed to share the sentiments of the vocalist as they joined in the singing, except for one teacher who was dancing with a particularly attractive girl.

' I don't agree,' Amadi heard him say to his dancing partner. ' After all the eye must eat first before the mouth. I can't live in the same house with a chimpanzee, no matter how exceptionally well behaved.'

' Why did you stop dancing so soon? ' Mr Chikwelu asked

Amadi as soon as the record was over and the master of ceremonies was changing the needle and winding the gramophone for the next record. ' You couldn't have felt tired so soon? '

' No,' replied Amadi. ' You see . . . well . . . she had a bad foot and . . . in my enthusiasm I stepped on it.' He eyed Nwakaego to see how she took the story, but her face was expressionless.

' Anything I can do to help? '

' No need to worry. She will be all right soon, though I am afraid it means she can't dance any more this afternoon. All the foot needs is rest.'

' *Ndo*, Miss Ikwuaju.' Without thinking, Nwakaego acknowledged his sympathy. The story worked well, especially when it turned out that the man they thought was Nwakaego's father turned out not to be her father but the Chairman of the Improvement League arriving for a discussion with the Headmaster. It also prevented anybody else that afternoon asking Nwakaego for a dance.

For Amadi, however, the afternoon held no further fun. Doubts which had begun to trickle into his mind following his first few meetings with Nwakaego, and which he had struggled to suppress, were now returning with redoubled vigour. What would his friends and colleagues at the University say if they heard of his attachment to a girl who had no mind of her own and who could not look her fiancé in the face?

As he rolled on his bed praying for sleep, he remembered an article in the *Crocodile*. It had appeared after an abortive attempt by the Students' Union to hold a Social evening with girls from nearby Secondary Schools. The article depicted young schoolgirls either looking at the ground, biting their nails, or turning their backs to the men when the men wanted to engage them in conversation. The conversation was often a one-way traffic; the men raised all the points and asked all the questions, the girls simply replied: Yes, Sir; no, Sir; I think so, Sir; I don't think so, Sir; or, I don't know, Sir. The article, after reporting on girls who even rose to offer their seats to men, concluded by asking how anyone could have expected the men to have enjoyed a social evening with such immature girls. And that had been the last social evening of this type in the University.

Nwakaego was beautiful in every sense of the word and had received excellent home training. Granted. But she was immature and there was a wide educational gap between her and Amadi. Things would be all right as soon as she obtained the Higher Elementary Teachers' Certificate—then she would be fit even for a Vice-Chancellor. But how soon would she attain that goal? With the best academic record, certainly not less than five and a half years, and longer if she suffered a setback. Was it wise to commit himself to a girl for that length of time? Perhaps yes, if the girl possessed exceptional qualities. Was there any guarantee that at the end of the long wait things would work out smoothly? What if he decided he did not like her any more? Or what if she decided at the end of it all that she preferred another man? It had happened to Simon, the Local Helper, and it had meant making a fresh start elsewhere. Of course, the parents could use their authority to prevent any such embarrassment but would he be glad to marry a girl either against her will or his own?

A voice spoke to him: 'You can't back out now. Remember you have all the time given your support. However long you may wait, Nwakaego will turn out to be what you make of her. Give her a fair chance. Show that you appreciate her problems. Don't compare her with Aduke . . .'

II

Some days after the party, Mazi Onuzulike again knocked on his son's door. It was 3.45 in the morning. Amadi opened up for him. After preliminary apologies for waking him up so early, his father hit the nail on the head.

'What is it I hear you have been discussing with your mother about Nwakaego?' he asked.

Amadi felt more at home with his mother than with his father; he found it easier to unburden his heart to her first, hear her views before both of them decided whether or not it was worth while taking the problem to his father. And so he had discussed Nwakaego with his mother before retiring for the night. He was surprised that she had spoken so soon to his father about it.

'I don't understand, Sir,' lied Amadi.

'Then everything is all right. I am sorry for disturbing your sleep. Let my words return to me, since what I thought I heard did not happen.' And he made a show of retracing his steps.

'No, Sir . . .' faltered Amadi, afraid to let this opportunity slip. 'Nothing has happened, Sir. It's only that I find it difficult to understand one or two things.'

'Like . . .?'

'Like . . . whether for instance I must marry Nwakaego?'

Mazi Onuzulike adjusted his heavy, locally woven, white covering cloth and sat down on the chair.

'Who is this Nwakaego you are talking about?'

'That one who comes here,' replied Amadi. 'The daughter of Mazi Nati Ikwuaju.'

'Oh, does she come here? Since when has she been visiting this house?'

'For a long time now.'

'I see.' His father appeared to be thinking. 'Tell me, what does she come here to do? To take fire?'

'No, Sir. If she came here for fire, the fire would go out before she reaches their house. She comes to visit us, and sometimes to stay for a time to help Mama.'

'How many other girls at Ezinkwo have come to stay with us and help your mother?'

'I can't think of any other.'

'Where is this Nwakaego now?'

'She must be in her father's house, Amadi replied evasively.

'You must be correct. That did not come to my mind.

But tell me, do you remember ever writing to me from the University about this Nwakaego? '

Amadi was becoming more and more uncomfortable about the turn the discussion was taking. He wrinkled his face and narrowed his eyes, in an ostensible effort to recapture past events; his father had given him a long rope.

' I have written so many letters to you and Mama since I left for the University that it is difficult to remember the letter you are referring to.'

' I can well understand. Sometimes I feel sorry for you book people. With all those books on that table inside your small head how can you still have space for small things like the contents of unimportant letters.' He adjusted his covering cloth and produced a crumpled letter which he had hidden away in the folds of the cloth. ' I think this is the letter I have in mind. Perhaps you would like to read it near the light to remember what you wrote in it.'

Amadi's hand was unsteady as he took the letter. He raised the flame of the hurricane lantern, spread out the letter and began to read. His father looked away from him; the gentle tapping of his left foot did not quite synchronise with the gnashing of his teeth. Amadi must have read the letter through at least three times before he returned it to his father.

' Was that the correct letter? ' asked his father. ' Old age is affecting me now and I don't know whether I brought the correct letter. Moreover, you know I cannot read.'

For some time neither of them spoke. Amadi turned the contents of the letter over and over in his mind. True, he had in that letter put up a strong case for sending his fiancée, Nwakaego, to the Secondary Modern School. He had, in fact, made it the only condition for marrying her. His father had carried out his instructions in spite of the additional financial burden on a farmer like him. Could he, Amadi, now have any justification for backing out?

' My ears are itching,' remarked his father, in an attempt to break the silence.

' Sir? '

' A proverb has a significance when it falls into the ears of the man who understands; when the good-for-nothing hears it he merely shakes the head till he staggers into the bush. To use proverbs on you young people of nowadays is as futile as running after an antelope. What I said was that I am anxious to hear what you have to say.'

' I have nothing to say, Sir, except that I don't think I shall be happy to marry that girl.'

' Why? '

' Because I don't think she is a suitable match for me.'

Mazi Onuzulike crossed his right leg over the left, gnashing his teeth as was his habit in moments of stress. He then spoke slowly.

' My son, you are still young, but not too young. You can now give a woman a child. It is true that the white man's education has brought a new kind of wisdom. We cannot run away from it, just as we cannot run away from the world. We must take what comes in our time. If, however, this white man's learning makes you forget the customs of the father and mother who bore you then it is not good learning.'

He paused to clear his throat. ' Now about Nwakaego. In my own time it was usual for parents to marry wives for their sons. My father was dead even before I tied cloth round my waist, but it was one of my uncles who married a wife for me. I have lived with your mother since then, produced you and trained you to what you are now, and I will continue to train you till you say you have learnt enough book. The Chairman of the Improvement League, Jeremiah the Churchwarden, Mazi Nati Ikwuaju, how can I attempt to count the sand on the ground? They all had wives married for them. Are they not happy with their wives? But the new world is coming; can we run away from it? Osita Umunakwe, in whose house you once stayed at Onitsha, he refused to live with the wife his parents found for him. The day his mother took the girl to him at Onitsha he would have taken them to the charge office, were it not that people intervened to prevent him. He would not give them shelter under his roof even for one night; it was Nwanneka's husband who gave them food and lodging that night. The following day they returned to Ezinkwo.

' You know what happened. Osita came home to block

our ears with talk about a man marrying the girl he loves. We did not know that one bitch as old as his mother had eaten his heart. In spite of every attempt to save the boy from the clutches of these township women who shake their bottoms from one side to another, he fell into the snare like an unobservant grasshopper. Today he is a useless man. After taking away all his money, she has run away to look for another prey. Osita cannot return to Ezinkwo in daylight.

' You know what else happened, only a year ago. Godwin Anagboso nearly died of " small cough ". Where is his wife now? Perhaps in Forcados, perhaps in Idah, who knows? Were it not for the advice we gave her, Godwin's mother would have died before her time. Godwin thought that only his eyes could tell which maize was ripe. He thought he knew everything about the girl he wanted to marry, simply because she was a seamstress in the town, a very wicked town, where he was the Local Helper. He was happy he had found a girl who could swell his monthly income of thirty shillings. It was after his wedding in the church that he realised that the wine was not as sweet as the wine tapper made him believe. His wife was wide awake. As soon as she suspected that her husband was losing interest in her, she put some medicine into his soup, and that's why Godwin nearly died of " small cough ". She left him last year, without leaving even one child for him.'

Amadi continued to listen. When he looked at his wrist watch his father took the hint.

' The second cock has crowed and I must give you time to snatch a little early morning sleep before day breaks. About Nwakaego. I do not have much to say. One proverb is sufficient for a wise man. Nwakaego comes from a good Christian home. Everybody knows that her father and mother have lived happily since they were married. She is a girl everybody likes. I have not heard of her passing any elderly person on the road without saying a word of salutation. She has been brought up very well, and under our own eyes. As you know, she has lived with us for many years of her life and your mother has taken every trouble to train her into a respectful and obedient wife for her son. We know the history of her ancestors which is as good as ours; there has been no trace of madness, white skin, or any other evil disease in their family. Her father and I have been friends from our youth. Her mother and your mother are very good friends. We believe that our children will live happily together.'

Amadi scratched his head at the easy logic.

' You have read more book than any other person, dead or living, at Ezinkwo, for which thanks be to God. If you thank the giver he will give more. I would not ask you to marry someone who has not even heard the school bells ringing. When you asked me to send Nwakaego to her new school, I agreed to do so even though many people thought I was foolish. I did so without counting the money it would cost me. I did so because I did not want to displease you. I hope you will not do anything that will make me look the daughter of a sheep. Learning is a very good thing, but book learning is not everything. It lies in your hands to turn your wife into whatever you want her to be. Did the daughter of Mgbokwu Anene ever step into a school? Does she not today speak and write English? It needs a hand to turn the forest into a dwelling place. The offspring of a snake cannot be short. A child who resembles neither mother nor father, was it thrown into the compound from the backyard? We know Mazi Nati, we know his wife, we like their ways. Nwakaego is a girl with plenty of commonsense, who is already taking after her mother. If you know you can't marry her because she is not teaching in the University, tell me. If you prefer those wise girls who help the gods to kill men, and whose family background you know nothing about, to a girl well brought up in a peaceful home, tell me. I have concluded my story and my mouth is tired.'

There was a silence. Amadi held his face in both palms and looked blank.

' My ears are itching,' reminded Mazi Onuzulike. ' You must have something to say, unless you feel I have been throwing up fodder.'

Amadi was burning to talk back. But he knew that in cir-cumstances like this he never emerged victorious. Almost every time he challenged his father's outmoded ideas in open conversation, he lost. His father had a way of making him feel that in spite of his vast book learning, there was still something lacking. This feeling of certain defeat had a psychological effect on him, it made him lose the trend of his airtight arguments.

'I have nothing to say now,' was all he could reply. He had a feeling of relief when his father left. He blew out the hurricane lamp and lay down. He was still awake when the Catechist rang the first bell for morning prayers, it usually went at 5.30; he did not hear the second bell.

His mother woke him up at eight o'clock to find out whether all was well. She was surprised he was still in bed when the children had all gone to school.

'Did you read book for a long time last night?' she asked. 'I have always told you to sleep now that you are at home. When you go back to that place you can begin again to eat kolanuts to keep awake.'

Amadi decided not to tell her anything about his early morning talk with his father, especially as he did not wish to be driven into further discussion at the moment. He would sleep on the matter and then write to his father from the University. There was nothing like a letter. He would arrange his points in a logical sequence, read the letter over for some days to make certain that his argument had no basket-like holes, before posting it to his father.

12

Amadi bowed low, at the same time describing a semicircle with his right arm, as Aduke opened her door for him.

'*Oliaku* . . .,' he began.

'Meaning what?' she interrupted, 'I've told you not to speak your barbaric language to me.'

' A peace maker doesn't use explosive words like barbaric, you know,' went on Amadi, smiling broadly.

' Oh, all right. Take a chair and finish your sentence.'

Amadi shut the door gently and took the chair offered him. ' As I was saying before I was rudely interrupted . . .,' he paused to laugh.

' Aren't you men tired of that joke? '

Every undergraduate knew the story. The Dean of the Faculty of Science was explaining a point at a meeting of the Faculty Board when a Professor, who was very unpopular with many of the students, broke in to give his own views. The Dean waited patiently for the intruder to conclude his speech. ' As I was saying before I was rudely interrupted . . .' and he continued his explanation from the point where it had been interrupted by the Professor. The story earned the rude Professor the nickname, ' As I was saying '.

' As I was saying,' repeated Amadi, ' *Oliaku* is the Ibo word for woman. Literally it means " consumer of wealth ".'

' I see! Of course, that's why our Hall is named Oliaku Hall. You took me by surprise.'

' Well, if I may be more serious, I have come to congratulate you on the magnificent role you played as a peace maker. Without people like you I don't know where we would have been today.'

Aduke was sitting on her bed, fidgeting with her nail file. ' Well,' she began, ' I must say it needed all my courage to decide to join the Peace Committee.'

The new academic year had brought new problems. The election of the President of the Students' Union had almost broken up the Union. Presidential elections usually sparked off a great deal of excitement, but never in the history of the Students' Union had five candidates been nominated for the office of President. What at first gave promise of a lively campaign soon took a different turn.

The morning before Election Day, three candidates notified the Electoral Officer that they no longer wished to contest the election. No reasons were given in their letters. At first, many took it that the three candidates had decided to step down for fear of losing their deposits. Then a handwritten article appeared on all student notice boards, entitled: DOWN WITH TRIBALISM. The writer observed that all three of the candidates who were standing down came from the same tribe.

'Why did they step down?' asked the writer. He went on to draw attention to a point which might not have been noticed by the electorate. 'Of the five candidates for the Presidential Elections four come from one tribe, and only the fifth belongs to the other major and rival tribe. The tribe with the four candidates realised that they would be beaten by the other tribe if they fielded their four candidates, as these four would merely split the votes that could have gone to a single candidate. Three of their candidates were therefore ordered to step down, leaving the candidate who was believed to be the most likely to win.'

This brilliant exposition achieved its aim. A notice-board battle ensued. Both typed and handwritten articles followed, a large number accepting the writer's observations, decrying tribalism as the bane of Union politics; while an equally large number expressed the view that the 'hypocritical' writer was doing the Union great injustice by crying 'fire' when there was no spark anywhere in the neighbourhood. They claimed that he would have done the Union—for which he professed so much love—greater good if he had boxed up his offensive pen. As he himself belonged to the tribe with the lone candidate many students could not accept his views as those of an impartial observer.

Events moved that day with the speed of lightning, so rapidly indeed that the Academic Registrar who had accepted appointment as Electoral Officer knew nothing about the squabble. He had gone to town that evening to see the film, *The Man Who Knew Too Much*. As he drove back from the cinema, near midnight, he kept marvelling at the amount of brain work, money and energy that went into a large-scale plot to overthrow established authority. As he took the final bend and made for his garage he was whistling the chorus:

87

Que sera, sera,
Whatever will be, will be;
The future's not ours to see,
Que sera, sera.
What will be, will be.

'Get up, chaps! I told you we wouldn't have to wait indefinitely. He's back at last.' There was a suppressed murmur as the fifty-odd undergraduates rose from the floor of the Academic Registrar's verandah, smacked the dust off their bottoms, lifted high their placards and moved slowly towards the garage. The Academic Registrar heard the suppressed murmur, stopped whistling and switched on the garage light. He started as he saw a man and a woman approaching him, followed by what looked like a fiery mob. His first impulse was to dash back into the garage and bolt the doors. But what would happen if the mob decided to bash in the garage doors? In any case, they were so near that they could surround him before he succeeded in locking the doors. Should he jump into the car and do a bolt?

He had taken two steps backwards when the woman greeted him. The voice was very familiar, and sounded reassuring. As she spoke, the man who walked beside her turned to the mob behind, asking them to stand where they were. The Academic Registrar unconsciously checked his own movements, and stared at the couple advancing towards him. The garage light soon showed him that they were two undergraduates he knew; he had often played cricket with the man, and had nursed a secret admiration for the girl. His heart was still beating like a drum inside him, and his thoughts were scattered like the seeds of a split oil bean pod as the two students approached him.

The girl was speaking. 'We are sorry, sir, to disturb you, but we have waited for you here since half past nine.'

The Academic Registrar's mind rapidly surveyed all the ground covered by his schedule of duties. Could this demonstration have anything to do with students who were frustrated by Heads of Departments not allowing them to proceed to Honours courses? If so, he thought, would they be appeased if I tell them that I will present their cases, with all the sympathy at my command, direct to the Vice-Chancellor instead of to the Council of Deans?

'We have come to you in your capacity as Electoral Officer. A big crisis looms over the Union, and you are the only authority capable of solving it. I shall now ask Mr Y—— the leader of the Minority Elements Association, to present our Resolutions.'

By this time, the fifty-odd undergraduates had surrounded their two leaders, their placards carried inscriptions such as: DOWN WITH TRIBALISM, UNITED WE STAND, DIVIDED WE FALL, ONLY MINORITY ELEMENTS CAN SAVE THE UNION. The Academic Registrar, who 'had breathed down' on realising that his life was safe, was still speechless. A mob was the last thing he expected to find on his doorstep at a time when he should be rounding off a busy day with a well-earned rest. If he had had the foggiest idea that this sort of reception was awaiting him, he could have spent the night somewhere else. His wife was safe in England and there would have been no questions asked.

The chief spokesman unfolded some sheets of paper and began to read:

'Our respected Electoral Officer. The Minority Elements in the Students' Union, that is the students who do not belong to the three major tribes in Nigeria, took the following resolutions, at a meeting held at 6 p.m. today in Lugard Hall quadrangle, and decided to pass them on to you for consideration and immediate implementation.' He then proceeded to read the twelve resolutions.

Many of the resolutions concerned themselves with the denunciation of tribalism. The most important resolution, as far as the Electoral Officer was concerned, was the one calling for a 'postponement of the Presidential Election, if the Union is to be saved from a major crisis'. The last resolution was no doubt calculated to win him over by flattering him:

'Finally, the Minority Elements Association unanimously agreed to place on record their appreciation of the impartial, understanding and painstaking manner in which you, Sir, have carried out your duties as Electoral Officer. The

Association would not be presenting these resolutions to you, if it did not believe that you would give them your character- istic mature consideration and then proceed to implement them. You are the last hope of the Students' Union and proper handling of this crisis will earn you an indelible place when the annals of the Students' Union are written.'

The Academic Registrar who had been turning over in his mind what kind of reply would be the most appropriate, rolled the sheets of resolutions into a paper cylinder.

'Ladies and gentlemen,' he began. 'I am grateful to you for the kind things you have said about me regarding my duties as your Electoral Officer. It is good of you to alert me about the impending Union crisis, even though one would have wished the warning had come a little earlier, considering that the election is due to start in about eight hours from now, and bearing in mind that the job of supervising Union elections is, strictly speaking, not one of my official duties.'

He paused for a little while, opened out the sheets of resolu- tions and folded them up again. 'I expect you want to hear my views on your resolutions?'

Everyone shouted 'Yes.'

'I am afraid it would be indiscreet for me to make any statements now. I will sleep on your resolutions which, as they were read to me, sounded very reasonable, and commun- icate my views to your leaders without undue delay.'

There was widespread muttering, and the Academic Regis- trar at once knew that his reply had not been easy to swallow. After a brief consultation with some of the students, the male leader spoke: 'The Association is very grateful to you, Sir, for consenting to think over our resolutions. Owing, however, to the urgency of the whole matter, the members would be indebted to you if you could indicate how soon your views will be made known.'

'I appreciate the position, and you can be sure you have my sympathy. Between you and me and this garage I would say at once—scrap the election and call for fresh nomina- tions!'

There was a loud ovation. 'Great! Great!'

The Academic Registrar had now taken a grip on his nerves.

'But, as an Officer of the University, I have to take many other factors into consideration before declaring my stand.' He paused. 'I never like making promises, as many of you may have found out. But I will make one promise to you tonight, and that is that I will give this matter the urgency it deserves. If the elections should be postponed, you will be informed before eight o'clock tomorrow morning when polling is due to begin. If you hear nothing from me before eight o'clock, you should take it that the elections will proceed as planned. Goodnight.'

As soon as he had seen the last of them disappear behind the thick lantana hedge surrounding his house, the Academic Registrar began to study the resolutions with the help of the garage light. He then drove off to report to his boss, the University Registrar.

'How many were there altogether?' asked the Registrar.

'I don't know the exact number. I guess not more than about sixty.'

'Oh, that's too small a number to bother about, judging from the total strength of the student body.'

'I had thought that myself. I wouldn't have knocked you up from bed if this group, though small numerically, hadn't contained quite a number of the more level-headed and reliable undergraduates on the campus.'

The University Registrar tried to think for a while. It was one of his characteristics never to give the impression that he talked without mature deliberation. It was usual for him to pause from time to time in any discussion, as if he was constantly turning the point at issue over and over in his mind.

'What do you advise?' he asked.

'That the election be put off till an atmosphere of calm prevails. This is the only way of avoiding the kind of ugly situation we had here some years ago.'

The Registrar brushed his hair with his right hand as he took a few paces in his sitting room, finishing up by digging both hands into the pockets of his dressing-gown.

'You know more than I do about these students. If you

are convinced that the course of action you propose is the best possible in the circumstances then go ahead. My policy in this University is to avoid any disturbances and allow the normal student to lead his University life in a peaceful atmosphere.' Pause. ' One last word. Make sure you study the Students' Union Constitution thoroughly to make sure that your proposed course of action doesn't conflict with any of its provisions. I hope I'll get around to reading it myself one of these days; my secretary left a copy in my tray about a month ago, but where's the time to read it? '

The election was put off. A notice appeared on all Hall Notice Boards before eight o'clock the following morning regretting that ' Presidential Elections due to be held this morning have been postponed owing to unforeseen circumstances. The new date will be announced before long.' The atmosphere, following the Electoral Officer's notice, was far from calm.

' What prompted you people to set up a Peace Committee? ' Amadi asked Aduke.

' Well, many of us believed the alarm was a false one. Some suspected the influence of external politics. As for me, I am not a supporter of anything that suggests divide and rule.'

' It's surprising that your Committee were able to handle the whole matter without the help of the authorities.'

' We tried to work hand in hand with them, but the Electoral Officer just couldn't understand the points at issue. So we told him we would try our hands and report back to him. It was he, in fact, who committed the first blunder, by putting off the elections without asking anybody's opinion.'

' But didn't I hear some students marched to his house with placards? '

' That's just the point. A few students describing themselves as Minority Elements march up to his house and present a series of disjointed resolutions; as a result he cancels the elections. Sometimes I can't understand these authorities. When you think their knees would quake as if they were rheumatic they stand as firm as the *iroko*, and when you would expect firmness they tremble like drenched rats.'

She went over the methods they had adopted. It was the belief of the Peace Committee that the Union was in great danger of disintegration if the elections were cancelled and fresh nominations ordered. Calling for fresh nominations might produce a worse stalemate, if it was true that the Yorubas and the Ibos had decided to wage war against each other. The Minority Elements would have the opportunity to present their own candidate, thus making the situation even more complicated. The Committee questioned the candidates who had withdrawn from the election and discovered that one of them had done so because his Professor, hearing he was a candidate, had warned him that few students could combine an effective Presidential role with a rewarding academic career; he had also told him that he was not among such rare students. The second withdrew because he preferred honourable withdrawal to a heavy defeat at the polls. The third stood down for no good reason, probably because it is sometimes fashionable to withdraw. All three were very helpful to the Committee and they agreed to stand for election if it was in the interest of the Union that they should do so.

The Electoral Officer was the final obstacle. The Committee thought he was trying to create a gigantic anthill where there was only a wasp's nest, in order to justify his action in cancelling the elections and for fear of incurring the displeasure of his superior officers. He gave himself away when the leader of the Committee, a History Honours student who had passed his Intermediate Bachelor of Laws—externally—before admission to the University, asked him whether, in his opinion, the three candidates could be regarded as having withdrawn from the election.

'What do *you* think?' The Electoral Officer asked the leader of the Committee evasively.

'In my opinion, Sir, these candidates have not withdrawn from the election.'

'Why do you say that?' He tried to hide his nervousness.

'Because the Union Constitution makes no provision for the withdrawal of candidates after nominations have closed.'

'What section of the Constitution are you referring to?'

'In actual fact, Sir, the Constitution is silent on this. It

93

defines the powers of the Electoral Officer very clearly, but nowhere does it empower him to authorise withdrawals, neither does it grant a candidate the right to back out. My Committee holds the view, Sir, that the three candidates should still be regarded as taking part in the election. And my Committee is glad to point out, Sir, that their views are supported by precedents in the national electoral regulations which make it impossible for anybody to withdraw from the election after nominations have closed. No member of my Committee, Sir, had been admitted to this University at the time the present Union Constitution was drawn up, but we have consulted one of its architects who is now a Senior Civil Servant in town and he says this was just the kind of situation that had been envisaged. Some students are in a hurry to get nominated, only to discover soon afterwards that they are not the darlings they thought they were. A day before the election they beg to withdraw " for personal reasons ".'

' Thank you very much, Mr er—I hope you will forgive me for being unable to pronounce your name! ' The Electoral Officer had now got over his nervousness. ' Between you and me and this table, I couldn't agree more with you. When my clerk showed me the letters of withdrawal I said to myself, surely there is no justification for this in the Constitution. But then I was told that such withdrawals were not unusual in this University. Having spent only a short while here, I thought I had better leave your traditions alone for the time being. No harm has been done yet. As a matter of fact, if I remember rightly, at no time did I write to accept the withdrawals. Moreover the election has only been postponed, not cancelled. I take it that you will sort things out with the Union and advise me on the date to proceed with the election.'

' That Academic Registrar is a big diplomat, you know,' remarked Amadi. ' When he sees black he turns black and when he sees white he turns white, and all the time he gives the impression he is on your side. That's what he did to me when I wanted to change my course to Medicine.'

' You read Medicine! ' Aduke asked derisively.

' Why not! I have a sound Science background for

Medicine, unlike you people who went to mushroom schools, where the students study science as they would literature.'

'If chaps like you who went to provincial schools brag like this, I wonder what people like us who schooled in Lagos should say! Anyway, as I was saying before . . . I cannot imagine you as Dr Chukwuka.'

'Why?' asked Amadi. 'Is it that the razor is not sharp or that Mgbeke does not know how to shave with it?'

'And what can that mean?' asked Aduke. 'Speaking your barbaric language again?'

'I am talking solid Ibo. May be you'll understand it one day.'

'Never!' replied Aduke.

'You can never be sure. But tell me, Aduke, would I have made a greater impression on you if I had been a medical student?'

'*Olorun ma je!* The kind of impression one of these braggarts made on a Form Three girl, telling her he was a " Thud Year Med'cal Stiud'nt ", in order to boost himself up. Some of us are not as naive as that. One decision I took a long time ago is that I will never be the wife of a medico.'

'And if I may ask, what kind of man do you hope to marry?'

'That's my secret. I'll know the man when I meet him.'

'And if I may pry into your secrets—as someone deeply interested in your personal affairs and welfare—would it be too much to ask whether you've met this lucky man?'

'It's news to hear that you're deeply interested in my personal affairs and welfare. Thank you. This, however, is a matter I feel competent to handle entirely by myself.'

13

The Presidential election over, calm once more returned to the University. The President was a level-headed undergraduate and his tenure of office was gradually coming to an end without a major crisis in the Union.

' Is this your eye, Ezenagu? ' asked Chima, standing by the Porter's counter in the Administration Building, waiting for the key to the lecture room where he often retired for his studies.

' Eye and its companion! ' replied Ezenagu humorously. He was amused by Chima's literal translation of the Ibo greeting for people who had not seen each other for a long time, and promptly reciprocated with a literal translation of the usual reply.

' You people appear periodically like the moon,' continued Chima. ' Frankly there are times I feel I shall merely be escorting some of you into the examination room.'

'Deceive me, deceive me, deceive me, deceive . . .' Ezenagu sang the only known line of a song popular among many undergraduates, although no one had ever taken the trouble to compose any more lines; it was usual to sing it up to the last ' deceive ' and then to abandon it there.

' You can't deceive me, I'm not the offspring of a sheep,' he went on, ' everybody pretends not to read, yet you can't find any of them in their rooms, not even at two in the morning. What are you doing here now? '

' Nothing,' replied Chima. ' Just loafing as usual; that's my hobby.'

The Porter emerged from the key room, holding a key in his hand. ' I tink na dis one. Make you go try am; if i'no fit open am, make you bring am back.' And he handed the key to Chima. ' Abi you don sign the book? '

Chima could not hide his embarrassment.

'I see how you loaf!' Ezenagu did not intend to let this opportunity slip through his fingers like agbono soup. 'I'm familiar with the tactics of die-hard swots like you. You hide yourselves in remote tutorial rooms where few people see you, and work there till your brain can't absorb any more. As soon as you return to the Hall of Residence, you give the impression you've not seen a book for the whole year and you brand the few students faithful to their rooms—swots. Isn't a swot the student who allows himself to be seen when he is reading?'

'Go on!' replied Chima. 'You have the mouth to say all this because you see me signing for the key to a tutorial room.'

'Actually my remarks are not directed at you personally, except that a proverb about a tattered basket always makes a man in rags nervous.'

'Alright, you win. Don't flog your point too hard. By the way, I hear the last issue of the *Crocodile* is the most pungent ever published.'

'Was it? I haven't seen it, and I didn't even know it had been published, especially after that threat by the University authorities that it'd be banned if its standard didn't improve.'

'Let the spirits judge which of us is the swot!'

'O.K. You've had your own back, and I hope you're now satisfied. Was the *Crocodile* the usual *Crocodile*? Or has it lost its bite?'

'The *Crocodile* of old! This time it bit both staff and students. Keep your ears near the ground and you'll hear the ballad of the ants!'

'Give me 'tory!' The two strolled into the Administration car park, with Chima doing the talking:

'The two friends, the Academic Registrar and the Professor of English, were bitten mercilessly. I was a bit sorry for the Academic Registrar. I am not sure he deserved the attack, although I have hardly had anything to do with him so I may not know enough about his diplomacy which the *Crocodile* described as cheap. He was portrayed as the kind of man who seems to be in agreement with opposing points of view. There were two cartoons of him—in one he was black in the midst of black persons, in the other he was white in a group of whites. The attack I enjoyed most was the one on the arch negrophobist.'

' The Professor of English? '

' Sure! You know he recently began to invite students to tea in his house, usually one at a time. Students soon saw through his trick. He was not interested in the students. He wanted to get some information from them. A student, using the pen-name "Detective", exposed him in an article entitled *Fear the Greeks and the Gifts they Bring*. You must read the article. Usually reliable sources say that the learned Professor has not issued any further invitations since then.'

' *Odi egwu!* ' Ezenagu listened more attentively.

' My friend Mr Chukwuka also caught it. Sometimes I wonder how these *Crocodile* men get their information.'

' These chaps are terrific! '

' What baffles me is how they got to know that Mr Chukwuka had a fiancée. A letter was addressed to Miss Owulo, Phone OHB 20, which is, of course, Miss Olowu, Oliaku Hall, wing B, room 20, and the writer signed himself "Sympathiser". Mr Sympathiser asked her whether she knew that the man struggling to establish himself as her "driver" had a fiancée who was merely waiting for him to graduate before she married him. Was she ready to engage in a boxing tournament with a girl far below her intellectual and social status? The last paragraph told her to ring NHA 74 and ask whoever answers the phone whether what he wrote was untrue. And NHA 74 is, of course, Niger Hall wing A room 74—Mr Chukwuka's room number.'

'Terrific! We certainly have budding Detective Inspectors in this University. Tell me, are Mr Chukwuka and Miss Olowu really serious? '

' Whosai! ' replied Chima. ' I warned that boy when Cupid was tempting him. I told him that he'd merely be trying to capture his shadow if he dreamt of chasing a Yoruba girl. He talked plenty of logic to me. I cited more dashing chaps who had tried and failed but the fellow sent me to market with silence, if you'll allow me another literal translation. He has now had it. Whoever tells a deaf man that disorder has broken out in the market?'

'You know one thing? This kind of attack can cement a friendship.'

'Oh yes,' agreed Chima. 'But you will also agree that it can break up a friendship. I am sure in this case it will break it, partly because it has never been strong, partly because the Yoruba men will have an excuse for redoubling their efforts at breaking it up. I shan't be surprised if Aduke's father arrives here any day. The bit about Chukwuka having a fiancée is partly true and partly untrue, but I don't doubt he's been giving Miss Olowu the impression that she's the only girl in his life!'

The radio in a student's room gave the Nigerian Broadcasting Service time signal for 9 p.m. The two men sprang up instinctively.

'Be seeing you!' They shouted simultaneously. Among the University students this usually meant 'Hope I shan't see you in the near future'. Each retired to his hideout.

14

As Aduke approached the University Park she began to wonder whether she was in her proper senses. This was the last week-end before the sessionals, her last sessional examinations before the finals at the end of the following academic year. The Professor of History was fond of referring to the results of each candidate's second year sessionals, particularly when the candidate was a borderline case. Instead of sitting tight in her room to revise her essays and the notes she had laboriously compiled from historical journals and documents, she was wasting the evening keeping an appointment with a man who was probably making a fool of her.

Her first reaction to the attack in the *Crocodile* was to ignore it. It was the work of jealous idiots who would only rejoice if they thought she was disturbed by it.

When first she began to notice Amadi's advances she did not take them seriously. Amadi was an Ibo, and there was no question of their ever getting married. No Yoruba girl of her acquaintance had done anything as crazy as marrying a ' Kobokobo ', the Yoruba's derogatory name for the Ibo, perhaps because the Ibos call the penny a *kobo*. If she had not brushed him aside completely, it was because she knew they could get nowhere. After Akin, the only serious boy friend she ever had, had broken his attachment to her, she had lost interest in any relationship that might lead somewhere. If Akin of all people could leave her, what chances of lasting success had she with any other man? ' Academic friendship ' was for her the safe target, and Amadi, a ' Kobokobo', seemed to fit the part admirably. She could allow him to take her to dances occasionally, and to pay her occasional visits, just enough of a relationship to keep other students away from her and leave her time to concentrate on her studies. There would be no problems involved in bidding him goodbye at the end of their career at the University. That was what ' academic friendship ' meant in undergraduate parlance.

She had no cause, therefore, to be angry with him even if, as the *Crocodile* columnist pointed out, he had a fiancée at home, though she thought it might be interesting to find out whether there was any truth in the allegation.

When she found herself walking to Niger Hall she knew she was acting against her better judgement. This was the third time she had found herself drawn to Amadi's Hall by a force beyond her control. The first had been the night Amadi was drunk at the dance; the second the morning after the dance. This time her courage amazed her. It was lunch time and the dining hall was full as she walked past. Many pairs of eyes followed each step that brought her nearer Amadi's room. She walked, she thought, like someone anxious to steal a hen in broad daylight as a reprisal for being wrongfully accused of stealing a chick in the dark.

As she drew near his room she could hear Amadi's voice. It was rather subdued, and she thought she also heard a woman's voice. She paused by the window trying to make out what they were saying but the discussion stopped abruptly. There was complete silence. When she advanced to the door to knock, she was no longer the high-spirited girl who had left Oliaku Hall determined to teach malicious students to keep their tongues in their mouths and their pens in their pockets.

The first knock had as much effect as if it had been delivered on the door of a deserted house. Her anxiety mounted. She knocked louder.

'Who's that?' Amadi asked, without coming to the door. Aduke's reply was a further knock.

'Why you dey make like small pikin? Abi you no know na person dey knock for door?'

Aduke could not identify the voice, but she sensed something unusual. The door opened just enough to accommodate Amadi's head. As soon as his anxious eyes fell on Aduke they lost their fire. His first impulse was to withdraw his head like a tortoise and bang the door. But that would be unjustified rudeness and would achieve no purpose. He opened the door a little wider, so that he could squeeze his body out of the room. He banged the door after him, and Aduke could see he wanted to shut her off from whoever was inside.

As they walked away from his room she prayed that none of the students would see them. The picture they presented as they walked silently down the corridor was far from the fine picture she had painted in her mind's eye as she had passed by the dining hall on her way to his room. The two of them walked like mourners. Amadi, his eyes focused on the ground, kept biting his lips, thinking rapidly, not of the *Crocodile* article, but of his more serious and immediate predicament. At the end of the corridor and in the seclusion of the staircase he stopped.

'Aduke, there is something very important I wish to discuss with you.' He still could not look her in the face.

'In connection with the very warm reception you have just given me? No, thank you!' With that, she moved on to the first step.

'Aduke, give me a chance. I know what you're thinking, but be sure you're not making a mistake.'

'I've too many bothers already to be worried by trifles. I'm sure this discussion is unnecessary. You're free to behave any way you like, and it's no business of mine how you enjoy yourself. After all, you're under no obligation to me, neither am I under any obligation to you.'

'O.K., we'd better leave it like that. Some students are at the foot of the staircase, and we don't want to furnish them with any more material for the *Crocodile*.'

'For all I care, they can write what they like.' There was an uncomfortagle pause. Amadi could see that Aduke was on the verge of flaring up and he did not want a scene. He spoke softly.

'Shall we meet at the University Park at five o'clock? That's undoubtedly the best meeting ground—quiet and isolated. It would be unwise for me to come to your room, as things are.'

'*You* can spend the whole day in the University Park; that's your own business. But you'll not find *me* there. I've got a room just as you have, and I intend to use it. I'll be seeing you.' And she walked off.

For fifteen long minutes Aduke sat on one of the improvised wooden chairs in the University Park, waiting for Amadi. She had arrived there at five minutes to five, and by ten minutes past five she was convinced she had made a fool of herself again.

She was very angry with herself. Was she the same Aduke who had spurned the inviting glances of her Lecturer in History of Political Ideas? Was she the girl who had successfully discouraged the most popular and sought-after Yoruba student in the University, a man not only a University Scholar but who was also Captain of cricket, Captain of football, Captain of athletics and Vice-Captain of netball? Had she not succeeded in isolating herself from men of her own kind in order to avoid further emotional upset? How could the same Aduke humiliate herself because of ordinary Amadi

Chukwuka—a 'Kobokobo' too for that matter! *Olorun gba mi O'* she muttered: 'God forbid!'

At a quarter past five Amadi had still not arrived. She found her saliva too hard to swallow. She rose, walked about aimlessly, almost unconsciously. When she stopped to take her bearings, she discovered that she was standing at the spot where she had once enjoyed a very pleasant picnic with Amadi and members of his Old Boys' Association. She immediately walked away from the spot, as if in protest. Her efforts to forget her cares by looking at the flowers proved abortive, and she decided to retrace her steps to her Hall. No, she would move across to the football field to watch a very thrilling league match which she had foolishly decided to miss in order to keep an appointment with an undeserving 'Kobokobo'.

'Miss Olowu!'

'Yes?' Turning back she saw the Hall Porter running after her.

'I slip one letter under your door. 'E come wen you no dey for Hall. 'E wait so-tee-e, 'e tire! So a giv'am paper wey 'e take write de letter for your room now now.'

'Thank you.' She knew the man the Porter was talking about. It was common practice for the Porters to use pronouns all the time when referring to any male undergraduate they felt was the regular boy friend of any girl in the Hall.

After overcoming the urge to tear up Amadi's note without reading it, she locked herself in, put on the light and sat on her bed to read the message.

When you dismissed the idea of visiting the University Park I thought you would wait for me in your room. After waiting here for a good thirty minutes (from 5 to 5.30), I took it that you were dodging me intentionally. Probably the episode this afternoon is working on you, or you are allowing your mind to be poisoned by hearsay. There is something very important I want to discuss with you tonight, as I may be leaving the campus tomorrow. I shall wait for you at Oliaku Lane, under the umbrella tree, between 8 o'clock and 8.15 to-night. I am sure you'll be there. Amadi.

'Nonsense! Me wait for him at Oliaku Lane! And give the silly man the chance to damage what is left of my name! Imagine his confidence—" I am sure you'll be there "! He will soon discover that he has not yet mastered me!'

As she walked to the dining hall she resolved not to step outside the hall that evening. The first consideration was her examination. All her classmates were hard at work. The dining hall was only half-full. Many girls were prepared to sacrifice their supper because of the waste of time involved in eating—the long wait for the people who sat at the high table, the sluggish and often cheeky service of the male stewards who would stick religiously to the order of the courses, refusing to serve the next one till everyone at the table had either finished or given up eating the course. To make matters worse, no one was allowed to leave the hall until a signal was given from the high table.

In between the courses, Aduke ran through the whole relationship between herself and Amadi. She could not escape from the thought that she liked Amadi. He was the kind of boy who could be friendly with a girl without making unreasonable demands. For that reason she felt safe with him. In her eyes he was different from other men, those ' adders ' who cannot imagine a boy-girl friendship without youthful excesses.

She also found Amadi intelligent in class, generally broad-minded and gentlemanly. She could not remember any occasion when he had embarrassed her in the company of other Ibo-speaking students. He had always seemed to place all his cards on the table till that *Crocodile* attack appeared. Was it true that he had a fiancée waiting intact for him at home, while she merely acted as a stop-gap for him at the University? She did not want to believe the insinuation in the *Crocodile* because she trusted Amadi who would surely not have hidden such a thing from her. After all, neither of them had ever proposed marriage to the other so there was no reason why he could not have told her he had a fiancée. Not that it would have affected their relationship, but at least it would have saved her this embarrassment.

She could not explain away the woman's voice she had heard

in his room that afternoon nor his refusal to admit her into the room. The disappointment in the University Park might be her own fault, but it aggravated the situation.

What was this important thing he wanted to discuss with her? His conscience was probably flogging him and he was cooking up something to tell her. What baffled her was his impending departure from the University. He had never cut examinations and it was incredible that he should contemplate leaving home a day before the sessionals. Perhaps she should meet him just to find out why he was leaving before the end of the academic year. Just that. If he wanted to discuss anything else she would walk away. She looked at her watch. It was ten minutes to eight. She went up to her room to fetch her pullover in case it became chilly later.

On her way out she met Chima at the Porter's Lodge. She was surprised to find him there; she could not remember ever seeing him in Oliaku Hall. He had always made a lot of noise about his fresh young girl at the School of Nursing, claiming that he would not waste his time on the academic women in the University.

In spite of his friendship with Amadi, Chima had not shown much kindness or courtesy to Aduke. He felt she was driving Amadi into committing a major blunder and, considered it his duty to drag him out by any means. He could not do this if he gave Aduke any sign of encouragement. Moreover, he had not forgotten that excuse-me-dance when she refused him as if he, Chima, was a leper or a ticket-collector. He was determined not to show any recognition of the friendship between Amadi and Aduke. Rather than smile at Aduke any time his eyes met hers, which was extremely rare, he tightened the expression on his face, as if he was having a painful time at the water closet.

Aduke knew that Chima had seen her, in spite of his effort to concentrate on the Visitors' Book. She smiled as she went past him. Then a thought came to her. Chima was widely recognised as Amadi's friend and he would know why Amadi was planning a sudden departure. She would forget about his rudeness and ask him for an explanation.

His reply might help her to decide whether or not to meet Amadi.

'Good evening.' Aduke spoke loud enough to make Chima realise she was addressing him. She felt like calling him Chima but the name stuck in her throat. She had never called him by name, not even by his surname, except in conversation with Amadi.

Chima ignored her and continued turning over the pages of the Visitors' Book. Aduke walked right up to him.

'Good evening,' she almost shouted. Chima turned in her direction.

'Ye . . . s?' His right hand was still holding the Visitors' Book as he gave her an uninviting look, the kind of look the School Captain might give to a little fag intruding into the Prefects' room at a time when the Captain was busy with important matters. It was quite evident that he did not wish to be friendly.

'Could I have a word with you outside?'

'What about?' asked Chima, and without waiting for an answer, went on: 'I have no intention of standing out there, and I can't imagine what we have to talk about. If there's anything you want to say, say it here.'

'It's nothing serious. Mr Chukwuka told me he might be travelling this week-end, and, since I saw you here, I thought I might ask you whether he has already left.'

'How am I expected to know?' asked Chima. 'You people don't realise I have more important things to engage my thoughts. I thought you knew his Hall and room number.'

Aduke decided not to accept the jibe. 'I'm afraid I don't.'

'Then find out!' With that he turned his attention once more to the Visitors' Book, and took no further notice of Aduke.

Fortunately no one was near to hear Aduke being snubbed or, as they would say when she was at school, to see Chima put an oversize coat on her, a coat of shame. She walked out into the cool air, in the direction of Oliaku Lane.

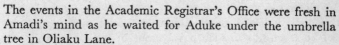

15

The events in the Academic Registrar's Office were fresh in Amadi's mind as he waited for Aduke under the umbrella tree in Oliaku Lane.

' What do you call yourself again? ' the Academic Registrar had asked him, a ball point pen in his hand ready to take down the stubborn name on paper.

'Amadi Chukwuka.'

' Not so fast. Let's have it all over again, this time slowly. . . How do you spell it? Fine. Now, which is the surname? '

' Chukwuka.'

' Sounds like I've had something to do with that name before. Now, Mr Chukwuka, do you know this girl? '

' I have met her before,' replied Amadi.

' Did you discuss anything with her? '

' Yes.'

' Could you tell us what you discussed? '

' Amadi cleared his throat.

' She wanted me to give her a note to the effect that I proposed to marry her, and, when I refused to do so, she threatened to report me to the Vice-Chancellor.'

' But what gave rise to the demand for the note? '

' She says I am the father of the baby she is expecting.'

' And aren't you? '

' No, I am not. I know nothing about . . .'

Sweetie and her mother broke in simultaneously: ' You are the one! You can't deny it.'

Amadi made no reply. The Academic Registrar looked confused. He knew the direction towards which the discussion was heading, and felt quite incapable of diverting or preventing it.

' Now, Mr Chukwuka, you say you are not responsible for the baby this lady is expecting? '

' Yes, Sir.'

' You lie! ' retorted Sweetie.

' You go see today! ' threatened her mother. ' If you think say you fit spoil other girls and run away, you no fit lef' my own daughter. You squirrel wey de chop palm fruit everyday, today you go knock your mouth for thorn! '

' Excuse me, Sir, could you ask them to stop using abusive words on me? '

' Well, ladies, I don't think any useful purpose will be served if we talk in such a way, out of turn, I mean.' He turned towards the expectant girl. ' Now, Miss, er, Sweetie, am I right? Can you repeat the story you told me in the presence of Mr Chukwuka? '

' Yes, Sir.' And, as she recounted the events of the past six months, she fidgeted with her fingers, pulling each finger of the left hand in turn. ' I first met Mr Chukwuka some time ago . . .'

' How long ago? ' interrupted the Academic Registrar. ' Could you be as exact as possible? '

' I don't remember the date, sir. It's more than six months ago. He came to spend a week-end in Lagos, with a man who lived in our yard. We didn't do anything then. When he returned to the University he wrote two letters to me, saying he loved me very much. I refused to reply. This is the photograph he sent me in one of the letters.' She produced a photograph of Amadi in undergraduate gown and mortar board.

Amadi stretched out his neck to see the photograph. It was his photo, all right. He stared at it, mouth open. Then he swung his eyes from the photograph to Sweetie.

' Do you say I sent you that photograph? ' he asked her.

' If you didn't, how did it get to me? '

' You dey min' that, liar? ' This from Sweetie's mother. ' Big big lie no reach am. Na we and you today? '

The Academic Registrar promptly intervened. ' Go on with your story, please, Miss Sweetie.' Amadi shook his head slowly.

'Nothing happened for a long time. Then about two months ago I visited the University. It was my first visit and I didn't know the road to the Zoo. I saw one student passing at a distance, and I moved towards him to ask him the way. When the student called me Sweetie, I was surprised to discover it was Mr Chukwuka. He said he would take me to the Zoo and round the University. I didn't want him to do so.'

'Why?' asked the Academic Registrar.

'Because I didn't want him to start enquiring why I didn't reply to his letters. And I feared that if he had the slightest chance he would try to use me.'

'Use you for what?'

'I mean he would try to take me to bed.' Sweetie lowered her eyelids. 'He tried to do it when we met in Lagos, that's why I disliked him. When he insisted on accompanying me, there was nothing else I could do. After seeing the Zoo he said he would take me to see a Hall of Residence. He took me to his room and asked me to sit on his bed. When I refused he forced me down. I just didn't know what to do. He left me in the room and went out with the key. I was so tired that I don't know when I fell asleep. What happened after that I cannot tell, except that I was surprised when in my sleep I moved and found him on top of me . . .'

'Excuse me, Sir,' shouted Amadi. 'I cannot bear this any longer. I'm going.'

'Why you dey move?' asked Sweetie's mother. 'Insect sting you for bottom? Sit down, my friend. When de ting dey sweet you, you no move!'

'Mr Chukwuka, I'm afraid I can't let you go, because I must hear your own version of the story.'

Amadi stood for a while and then warmed his seat once more on the chair.

'Have you finished?' asked the Academic Registrar, looking at Sweetie.

'Yes, Sir. I know he will deny. Mama, give me that bag, let me show him the pantie I wore that day, how he soiled and tore it in our struggle.'

'I wouldn't worry about that,' cut in the Academic Registrar. 'Now, Mr, er, what have you to say?'

' Nothing, Sir! '

' You no talk? Talk now! True word no get reply! '

Amadi looked at Sweetie's mother, shut his eyes derisively and turned away.

' When eye look pot finish, make 'e take am break for ground.' She also shut her eyes derisively, simultaneously producing a contemptuous clicking sound with her tongue.

' Surely you must have something to say, young man,' pleaded the Academic Registrar. ' Do I take it then that you accept all she has said? '

' She knows she is lying.'

' Did you see her the day she visited the Zoo? '

' Yes, Sir.'

' Did you take her to your room? '

' I did, but at her request and against my wish. Practically every student who spends his vacations in Lagos knows her, and I knew that if she was found in my room students would draw conclusions. But she said she was dying of thirst, her legs were weak, her feet sore and she needed a little rest. I took her through the back entrance, to avoid undue publicity, left her in the room and went to the dining hall to fetch iced water. I pocketed the key to make sure that no student entered the room in my absence. When I returned with the water, I was shocked to find her lying stark naked on my bed, with her eyes closed, even though I knew she wasn't asleep. I told her to behave herself but she pretended not to hear. I knew that if I kept looking at her I might be tempted, so I picked up a book and tried to ignore her. But she wouldn't let me. She pulled me to the bed and tried every device to break down my resistance . . .'

' Na lie O! Make you no believe am O! ' shouted Sweetie's mother.

' Please, madam, give him a chance to speak,' intervened the Academic Registrar.

' Much as I am tempted to do so,' continued Amadi, ' I shan't go into the sordid details. It's enough to say that she finally succeeded in breaking down my resistance, especially after she began to create a scene in the room, and I was anxious to avoid providing material for eavesdroppers. But if she's honest with herself, she'll tell you that she got very angry with me because I let myself go while she was trying to show me the way in. What happened could not give any girl a baby.'

'That's not true,' protested Sweetie. 'You entered fully.'

'I don't need any more details,' cut in the Academic Registrar. He knew the discussion could lead them nowhere. After a moment of thought he excused himself from the room for a few minutes. When he returned he addressed Sweetie's mother.

'Now, madam, what help do you want from the University?'

'My daughter lef' Teacher Training College last December. Gov'ment bond hol' am for two years. Now as 'e get belly when 'e never get husband, dem go sack am from teaching and ask am to pay for bond wey 'e break, unless dis man giv' am paper say him wan' marry am.'

'Is that all?' asked the Academic Registrar.

'Yes, Sir,' replied Sweetie's mother. 'Me I no get money chop garri who sai I fit get sixty pounds pay bond?'

'I have no intention of marrying your daughter. If you like you can go back and make up more stories.'

'Who wants you to marry her?' asked Sweetie. 'Are you up to the shoe lace of men who have been begging to marry me? Nonsense!'

'Make you no min' am. Who wan' make you marry my daughter? Me I no go want liar like you for son-in-law! I no go let any man wey no love my daughter marry am. No fear.'

'So you don't really want this man to marry your daughter?' asked the Academic Registrar. 'You only want a note from him, declaring his intention to marry her, so as to save her job and the sixty pound penalty she would be required to pay the Government for premature resignation. It does not matter to you whether in the end he refuses to marry her? My young man, you should go and write the note and give it to them. If you do that, the matter will end here. O.K.? We've all been boys and girls in our day!'

'I am sorry, Sir, I don't think I can give them any such note.'

'You will. If there is anything the University is expected to teach you, it is to accept responsibility for your actions. I have listened carefully to both sides of the story. Essentially, both of you agree that something transpired. You differ on the details, which I consider immaterial. Well, madam, you can go with him and he will give you the note. That's all I can do for you.'

'Thank Sir.'

'Thank Sir.'

'Not a bit. It's a pleasure!'

They had followed him to his room for the note which he refused to write. It was at this juncture that Aduke had knocked on his door. After that events had moved very rapidly. Sweetie and her mother, on leaving his room, went to the Academic Registrar's house to report the outcome. The Vice-Chancellor was consulted. Amadi was asked to leave the University within twenty-four hours, and to stay away for the rest of the term for failing to carry out 'the lawful commands of an officer of the University'.

He lost all self-control as Aduke stood beside him under the umbrella tree. She knew from his unsteady voice and his sniffs that he was struggling not to sob.

'The thought of it . . .' muttered Amadi. 'To move from one scandal to another. How can I face my parents? What will I tell them? How can I go through my remaining year in the University with such a scandal around? How can I face you, Aduke?'

'I wouldn't worry about Aduke if I were you. After all, there's nothing between us and you owe me no explanation. I only hope this doesn't get near the ears of your fiancée.'

Amadi thrust her off gently. 'Aduke, I didn't call you out here to poke a stick at my ulcer. If that's what you've come for, I beg to wish you good night and goodbye.'

'What do you think I've come here to do?' she asked. 'To rejoice that I am a much greater fool than anyone could ever imagine? Early today it was something about a fiancée at home. Now it is a beautiful Lagos girl who has never featured in any of your conversation, suddenly expecting a baby from you.'

'Aduke! Aduke!'

Amadi was alarmed at the manner in which she suddenly left him. By the time he had pulled himself together she had disappeared. He stared in the direction of Oliaku Hall. In a dramatic manner she was gone, the one person he hoped would believe his innocence. Gone, convinced that he, Amadi, was just like other irresponsible 'Adders'. Gone, leaving him under the umbrella tree on a cold dark night, alone and miserable. It took him some time to suppress the lump in his throat that was making him uncomfortable. He counted his steps to Niger Hall in an effort to find an alternative occupation for his thoughts.

16

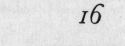

'Mama, Amadi has returned.'

'Shut your mouth,' Amadi's mother rebuked her young son, Moses. 'I have warned you several times to stop calling your brother's name unnecessarily; you will only make him sneeze frequently, wondering who could be calling him from afar. In any case who asked you to come to the farm? Have you finished cracking the heap of kernels I asked you to crack?'

'Mama, it is Amadi who sent me to tell you that he has come home.'

Mrs Chukwuka saw from Moses's face that he was not playing pranks. She walked nearer him.

'Are you telling the truth?'

'Yes, Ma.'

'Did you see him with your eyes?'

'Yes, Ma.'

' Is he well? '

' He does not look sick.'

' Papa Amadi! Papa Amadi! ' She not only shouted for her husband but ran towards him.

' What is the matter? ' he asked.

' I think you received a letter from Amadi last week. When did he say they will close for their holiday? '

' After this coming Saturday has passed, the next one. Is that why you are shouting at me? '

' Moses has just come to tell us that Amadi has returned.'

' True? Where is he? Moses! Come here. Did you see Amadi? What was he carrying? '

' Good afternoon, Sir. He was carrying his leather portmanteau and his small bag, Sir.'

Mazi Onuzulike abandoned the yam tendrils he was disentangling and let his mind run loose.

' Missus!' That was often the way he addressed his wife.

' Sir? '

' A corpse is not a new thing to the soil. There is nothing that can happen in one part of this world which has not happened somewhere else. Since we cannot run away from the world we must face whatever comes our way. Moses, you say he talked to you? He sent you to tell us that he has returned? '

' Yes, Sir.'

' Thank God he is alive. Life is the important thing. Missus, take the basket and some cobs of maize and go with Moses. I shall follow behind with the food for the goats.'

Mrs Chukwuka walked home with wooden legs. She became more upset when she knocked the big toe of her left foot on a concealed stone. The left foot, it was surely an evil omen. She did not believe Moses's story, though she hoped it would be true. She feared that her son was dead and dreaded the thought. Instead of going straight home she made a detour. Her object was to pass by the market. The truth would come out there. If her son was dead, it would be difficult to conceal the news in the faces of the Postal Agent, the tailors and the seamstresses.

They greeted her with their usual warmth, except that the

Postal Agent beckoned to her to ask why Amadi had returned almost two weeks earlier than he had said in his letter to Mazi Onuzulike.

' I have not seen him yet. He sent this boy to tell us that he has returned, and I am just from the farm and have not reached home.'

' Didn't he tell you he was returning today? '

' I don't remember. He may have told his father.'

She felt much lighter as she walked home. Her son was still alive. That was all that mattered.

Amadi did not receive a hero's welcome, nor had he expected one. He would have liked to have returned after dark, to avoid meeting many people. That was why he decided to board *Early Bird*, the lorry reputed to be the slowest on the Ezinkwo to Onitsha road, and which never reached Ezinkwo while chickens were still moving about. Unfortunately, he learnt that the Police had ordered the decrepit old lorry off the road. When he arrived at the village, instead of rushing out to embrace him, people stopped to look in his direction as if he were a ghost. Those who shook hands with him took pains to find out from him whether all was well. He began to wonder if the news of his affair with Sweetie had preceded him.

Even his mother did not give him her usual warm welcoming embrace, nor did she rush into the compound as she usually did. She dropped the basket of maize in front of the kitchen and walked towards his one-room house with great solemnity.

' Amadi! '

' Ma! Good afternoon, Ma.' He came out of the house. Mother and son stood in front of each other, Amadi looking at a hen digging up an earthworm for its dinner, assisted by half-frightened chicks which pecked at the writhing worm and immediately retreated in case the worm decided to retaliate.

' Have you closed for your holiday? '

' Yes, Ma.'

' But in the letter you wrote to your father some days ago, you said you will close the Saturday after coming Saturday.'

'Yes, but there was a sudden change in plans and the authorities asked us to leave earlier.'

'So you mean there is nothing wrong?'

'No, Ma.'

'Aha! Let me breathe down. Since Moses came to the farm to announce your arrival my heart and your Papa's heart have been hanging on the ceiling. You know, this is the second time you have come home without writing to warn us. The first was when they refused to allow you to train as a doctor. This time we could not understand what was wrong.'

Amadi regretted he had not broken the ' Nsugbe coconut '. What was the point in pretending that all was well when he knew he was lying? The words were heavy in his mouth. All through the long journey home he had formulated different methods of approach. None appeared satisfactory to him.

He told the same story to his father.

'What was this sudden change?' his father had asked.

'They wanted to re-decorate the Hall of Residence.'

'Why couldn't they wait for two weeks?'

Amadi realised how unconvincing his lie was, and remembered that his father, though illiterate, was intelligent.

'There is a very important conference to be held at the University. People are coming from all parts of the world— from *obodo oyibo* [the United Kingdom], Germany, America and other places. The authorities want the whole University to look attractive so as to give a good impression to the foreigners.'

'I see. What about your examinations? You said in your letter that they would start today.'

'The time was also shifted. We finished them two days ago.'

'How did they go?'

'I tried my best. The results are not yet out because we left for the holidays almost as soon as we left the examination room. Anyway, this is not an important examination.'

'If I had had the chance you boys now have, I would not be at Ezinkwo praying to beetles to spare my yams.'

Amadi retired early, ostensibly on the grounds that he was tired, but in fact because he wanted to prevent the curious neighbours who came to welcome him from finding out why he had returned unheralded. When later he heard a knock on his door he was not certain whether he had had any sleep. He looked at his watch; it was ten past three. He knew who was knocking—he opened the door and his father walked in.

' My son, I am sorry to knock at your door at this time of the night, especially after your long travel. But, as I must have told you before, if you were living at home this is the time we would whisper together free from any interruption. Also this is the only time I can talk with you. You people sleep like the white men; by the time your morning breaks I have done a lot of work on the farm.'

Amadi listened to his heart beat.

' Do you and Nwakaego write to each other from time to time? '

' Yes, Sir.'

' When did you hear from her last? '

' Not a long time ago.'

' I love that girl intensely, so much so that I love even her footprints. There is nothing like marrying a girl from a good family, a girl who has kept to herself. She comes to her husband's house with fresh blood. Once husband and wife meet, God sends them a healthy child. Unfortunately, the white man is changing everything. Young boys now prefer these harlots who have sold shame in the market. Every man they meet knows their secret parts. Before they marry they have committed abortion many times, sometimes by drinking ink, sometimes by eating too much pepper. The unlucky man who brings that kind of woman into his house is only setting his own house on fire. They are the type that visit every herbalist before they become pregnant. Some of them come to eat down a man, after which they run away with his belongings. Do you know Ikeme Nwoye? '

' No, Sir.'

' You won't, because he is not a native of Ezinkwo. He comes from Ndikpa, but he has not returned to Ndikpa since you were born. Why? He went to work in Lagos and, in spite of everybody's warning, he decided to marry one of these serpents. He said he would not marry a bush girl from Ndikpa who could not go to dance at the club with him. He wanted to marry a Lagos girl who knew how to make him happy. He is a dead man, even though his skeleton still staggers about in Lagos. He does not have the face to return to Ndikpa today. The woman put medicine in his food: after eating it he could not refuse anything she asked of him. His old mother died five years ago of heartbreak: the only son on whom she depended to support her in her old age had neglected her completely. His wife did not even allow him to write to his mother or to send her money. He was the first son of Ndikpa to get Government work in Lagos, and his people were very proud of him. Today, no mother or father at Ndikpa will allow his son to go to Lagos for work. You don't know how your mother and I have been thanking God that you have not fallen into the hands of those devils. Anyway, a child who does not resemble its mother must resemble its father.'

He looked at Amadi, who could no longer conceal his confusion.

'You seem to be sending me to market with silence. Am I to take it that you do not agree with what I am saying?' he asked.

Amadi became increasingly uncomfortable. He could not understand why the discussion should be moving in this direction. Did his father know? Whether it was purely coincidental or not, he decided the time had come to break the 'Nsugbe coconut'.

'Well, Papa, I have been wanting to say something . . .'

Mazi Onuzulike listened intently. Deep down in his inside he knew something had gone amiss, but he could not figure out what it was. Somehow he had found it difficult to believe the story about the Halls being painted before the end of term and when he lay down and closed his eyes he could not sleep. Had his son failed an examination? He had been a very brilliant boy since his childhood. Had he stolen? That was impossible. As an infant he was not caught even once stealing meat from the soup pot. Only on one occasion did he return from school with a ruler that did not belong to him, but he received three strokes of the cane on the bottom for that and had never repeated the mistake. What else could he have done?

He waited for his son's story as anxiously as he had waited in his *obi* when his wife was in labour shortly before the birth of Amadi—afraid that what came would not be what he desired and at the same time hoping for the best. As soon as Amadi mentioned a woman's name he knew that what he had dreaded most had happened. He began unconsciously to gnash his teeth. He did not utter one word until Amadi had finished. Even after he had finished the blank look remained on his face and there followed a tense uncomfortable silence, after which he stood up and made for his own room.

At first, Amadi felt considerable relief at having broken the ' Nsugbe coconut '. A great deal of his unhappiness all the way from the University to Ezinkwo had been over how to break the unpleasant news to his parents. Fear of their reactions had been of secondary importance. That was why he felt relieved even though he knew the matter was not yet closed. His father had left without saying a word and Amadi knew what that meant, just as everyone at Ezinkwo knew that blinding flashes of lightning meant an impending storm. The impending storm could not, however, keep Amadi awake; he slept as an escape from it.

In his sleep he dreamt of a great storm. The wind blew with terrific force and the rain lashed the roof and the walls. All the windows were closed and everyone sat uneasily, shutting their eyes tight at each angry flash of lightning and producing the customary sound with their lips, the sound which was believed to protect the person who produced it from the thunder that followed—the ' gun of the sky ', as it was generally called. No one who made this sound had ever been killed by thunder at Ezinkwo. In his dream, Amadi could hear his mother remark that it was the most severe storm she had seen in her life. The words had not left her mouth when a tremendous crash was heard. Everyone started, holding his heart in both hands. Was it the roof of the village church or the large *iroko* tree whose falling leaves always provided fun for the children each Christmas season? The darkness outside was impregnable, except when the lightning slashed through it. Amadi volunteered to brave the darkness and the rain to see what had fallen.

He rose from his bed, walked to the door and pulled the bolt. The door opened, and he staggered back as he walked into his father who was entering the room. He rubbed his eyes, trying to place himself.

'Are you off your mind?' stormed Mazi Onuzulike. 'You have kept me knocking on this door for a long time. Even the civet cat does not sleep like that!'

They sat down, Mazi Onuzulike on the chair and Amadi on his bed. After a brief silence, Mazi Onuzulike spoke.

'Amadi. My words are few. You have painted my face and your mother's face with charcoal. I have always pulled your ears with my hand and warned you to beware of these township girls. I have begged you to put your sword in its sheath because one day you will be tired of lying down with a woman. I and your mother were anxious that you should marry quickly because we feared that young men of today find it difficult to control themselves. Nwakaego is waiting for you, just as the water in the broken pot waits for the dog to drink it. But I knew your mind was not on Nwakaego. You wanted someone who had gone to England to study, somebody who could speak English to you. Now that you have eaten the thing that has kept you awake let me watch you sleep! Now that you have fallen into the hands of those township girls who help the gods to kill, you will understand why I have been warning you to avoid women as you would avoid lepers. When a child eats a toad, it kills his appetite for meat.'

Amadi decided to break in. 'Papa, I know I have behaved stupidly, but I want you to believe me: I am not responsible for the child. You know I have never told you a lie, and no one learns how to use his left hand at old age.'

'Yes, I know you have never told me a lie. But it is only Mary the mother of Our Lord Jesus who became pregnant without lying with a man. When Okeke Mgboli was accused of giving a child to one of his father's young wives, he was prepared to swear by the god of thunder that he did not touch the ripe apple. He said he was accused falsely because he was seen helping the woman when the cloth she tied fell off her waist. When the child was born the face showed who the father was.'

' Papa, does it mean you do not believe me? '

' I have not said that I disbelieve you, neither have I said that I believe you. What I know is that you have been sent away from the University for making a township girl pregnant. And that you have painted my face with charcoal. Nothing so shameful has happened to me all my life. With what face can I confront Nwakaego's father and mother? How can I go up to the Improvement League to say that my son and the hope of the whole town has been sent away from the University because of a prostitute? Amadi, the more I see you in this house the more my heart breaks into pieces.'

When Amadi left Ezinkwo early that morning he did not know his destination. It was not until the lorry stopped at Onitsha motor park and all the passengers got off that he realised he did not know where he wanted to travel to, a heavy drop trickled down each cheek as he took his bearings. Here at the motor park he stood, the pride of Ezinkwo, the first son of the soil to enter a University, the man who held the magic wand that could transform Ezinkwo overnight, the man on whom the scanty savings of the villagers had been spent. Here he stood, alone, rusticated by the University, spurned by Aduke and unaccepted at Ezinkwo, even in his father's house. For one moment the River Niger, gleaming in the distance as it reflected the rays of the early morning sun, appeared an easy end to his problems. In desperation he walked towards it.

17

News spreads fast at Ezinkwo, as fast as the gong of the town-crier's *ogene*. Word soon went round the village that Amadi Chukwuka had put a girl in the family way. Some called her a Yoruba girl, some a Calabar girl, some a prostitute from *Mba mmiri* which was usually associated with 'mammy water' and where, from time to time, girls appear to men in the guise of beautiful maidens. People called at Mazi Onuzulike's house to express their concern and sympathy.

Mazi Nathaniel Ikwuaju, Nwakaego's father, was one of the early callers. ' In-law,' he began, ' what is this I am hearing?'

' It is the sign of the times, and we cannot run away from the world.'

Mazi Nati lowered his voice. ' But, in-law, do you mean to tell me that the story I heard is true? I cannot believe it. No, I cannot.'

' I myself did not believe it when I heard it. At first I thought I was in a trance. I never expected a son, born to me, to be connected with such a shameful thing. But don't we have a proverb about the dry, withered tree which everybody expected to fall, surviving the storm while the young lively tree crashes down? '

Mazi Nati shook his head slowly from side to side, at the same time snapping his fingers. ' In-law, this thing has not given me the mouth to talk. A boy on whose head such uncountable sums of money have been spent since his childhood ending up in such a way, without being in a position where he could give even a head of tobacco to his father or soap to his mother, all because of these women who help the gods to kill. It is like a hungry man washing his hands to crack a palm kernel only to find the kernel falling off the stone and being carried away by a chicken.'

' When a man of my age weeps you can be sure that the cause is serious. My son has made me weep, something I did not do when thieves removed almost everything I owned in this world five years ago. You remember? '

' Please don't dig up that old incident. In-law, what do you think the Improvement League will do about the matter? '

' Will I sniff my palm with my nose to know? I have told my he-goat son that he must pay back to the Improvement League all the money they threw into the river because of him before he enters my house again. And he must also pay back to me all the money I have spent on him. If I had used all the pennies I have spent on him to look after myself, I would not be moving in rags today like Jadum the madman. I did not mind spending the money because I believed my son would help his brothers and sisters and look after me and his mother in our old age.'

Mazi Onuzulike paused for a pinch of tobacco. He returned the snuff-box to Mazi Nati who tucked it away in the folds of his wrapper.

' In-law,' resumed Mazi Onuzulike. ' It is not the disappointment to the Improvement League that makes me weep. It is not even the disappointment to myself. Thanks to God above, I am not the poorest man at Ezinkwo and I can always feed myself and my wife and children. As for the training of the children, tomorrow is pregnant and nobody knows to what it will give birth.

' In-law, do you know what made me weep? When I remembered our daughter Nwakaego.'

Mazi Nati suppressed a sigh and gritted his teeth. That was why he had come to Mazi Onuzulike, although it would have been indiscreet for him to introduce the discussion. But now that Mazi Onuzulike had called the evil disease by name, he had no mouth to talk, not knowing how to begin.

Mazi Onuzulike continued. ' This is not a matter to discuss while we stand. It is something we shall come to your house to discuss fully. I remember clearly the day Nwakaego was born, how I and my Missus took to her and declared that we would like her as a wife for our son. Since then every person has steered clear of her, regarding her as our wife. She herself has come to look on us as her parents and we have found her an excellent daughter. If anybody had told me that it would all end like this I would not have believed him. I was so certain that everything would end well that I did not attach any importance to the fact that I hit one of my left toes on a stone, the day I was going to your house to rub the white chalk announcing Nwakaego's birth. All I knew was that I had experienced no stumbling block in my long period of comradeship with you, and I did not see any reason why my son and your daughter could not live happily together.'

'In-law,' Mazi Nati spoke slowly, 'as you said, this is not the kind of matter to discuss in a hurry; there is therefore no need to speak in a rush. What has happened has happened. It may be that God with His special eyes saw something bad coming which we could not see. Did not our fathers pray that the pot of palm wine, which would bring disagreement between in-laws, should break on the road without ever reaching its destination?'

A brief silence followed.

'In-law,' began Mazi Nati, 'what is going to happen about the girl to whom your son has given the child?'

'That is not a matter to be referred to the oracle for solution. He will marry her.'

'Where is her home town?'

'I do not know. My son has never spoken to me about her. All the time I had been warning him against those women who have sold shame in the market, he has always sworn that he had nothing to do with these women.'

'Do you mean you will leave your son to marry a girl you do not know, a girl whose parents and family history you do not know, a girl whose conduct you have not observed?'

'In-law, what do you expect me to do? A child is a blessing from God which we cannot refuse. Any man who decides to taste the forbidden fruit must be prepared to face the consequences as Adam and Eve did. Father Tortoise has nothing to add to that.'

Mazi Nati made no comment. The fact that the most eligible son-in-law at Ezinkwo had slipped through his fingers like the eel did not blind him to the fact that Mazi Onuzulike spoke the truth. He knew that at Ezinkwo any man who gives a woman a child marries her, although this hardly ever happened outside marriage except when a woman was authorised by her family to bear children for that family, and this only happened when the family concerned was in danger of extermination for lack of male offspring.

Mazi Onuzulike was an unhappy man. He was one of the Church leaders at Ezinkwo, widely accepted as such for miles around. His strong views on morality were well known. On one occasion he had said he would disown any of his daughters if he caught her dancing with a man. No boy was allowed to pay useless visits to his daughters and none of his children were allowed to step out of his house after dusk. The other children of the village often teased his own by saying they retired earlier than chickens. But the Catechist and the Pastor always cited his children as examples of those who were brought up in the fear of the Lord. Amadi was the darling of many, not only because he was the symbol of learning at Ezinkwo, but because in spite of all his learning he was humble and respectful to elderly people. His popularity was evident from the fact that his father and his mother were designated ' Papa Amadi ' and ' Mama Amadi ', as if they were not also Papa and Mama to their other children.

Mazi Onuzulike himself was an example to his children. He was never involved in any scandal and he was a very faithful husband to his wife. To him, sex was not invented by God as a source of pleasure to man. Even a married couple had no right to entertain each other sexually. They slept in separate rooms most of the time, the man ' visiting ' his wife only when they needed a child.

Amadi had made it possible ' for goats to eat palm fronds off his head '. He had dragged him in the mud and given the village gossips something to talk about. How could he stand before his people another day to decry immorality unless he made an example of his son? How could he in one breath invoke the wrath of God on prostitutes and other dangerous township women, and in another welcome one of them to his house as a daughter-in-law? How could he encourage his son to disclaim his child, his own blood, his own first-fruit? For who knew whether such a child might not grow up one day to take up arms against his own father without knowing it?

No, he needed no oracle to point out the way. Amadi must accept full responsibility for his indiscretion. He must marry the girl, but he must not bring her to his house. He had broken his father's commandments and he was no longer his father's son. Like the arm about to lead its owner to damnation, and notwithstanding the pain, he had to be cut off.

But not very easily. Mazi Onuzulike loved Amadi. He was proud of his academic record, and proud to be the father of the first son of Ezinkwo to enter a University. He had closed his ears to every suggestion that Amadi should begin to earn a living immediately after leaving the secondary school. He had faith that one day all would be well. He did not mind even if he went naked in order to save money for his son's education; one day God would send him clothes in superabundance. The days of expectation were close—only round the bend of the road. One more year and his son would own the first car at Ezinkwo, and he would be the father of a District Officer. Could he shut his mind to all this? Could he cut off his nose to spite his face? His second son was still in primary school. Must he wait for him? How could he be sure that he also would not prove a disappointment at the last moment?

Then there was the problem of his wife. He had consulted her before dismissing Amadi from his house. It was she who had described Amadi as a boil that had developed in a most embarrassing part of the body. But now Amadi's departure from Ezinkwo seemed to have sapped her dry. She would often forget whatever she was doing and look lost in thought. Whenever someone called her back to the world of reality, she would heave a heavy sigh and return to her work. She did not wish to hear Amadi's name mentioned, yet she could not get him off her mind. She lost control of her feelings the day Nwakaego, home for the August holidays, came to greet her. She burst into tears and the sight of her sent Nwakaego weeping too. Neither consoled the other. They each understood why the other wept and there was no need after that to discuss the matter.

'Mama, I only came to greet you and to tell you that I am home on holiday.'

'Thank you, my daughter. You have done very well. What about your studies?'

'They are going on well, Ma. We have taken our mid-year examination.'

'Did you do well?'

'I think so, Ma, even though we have not been given the result.'

'My daughter, God who fights for us even in our absence will see that you pass. Your brain is open.'

Nwakaego made no reply. After a brief pause she stood up to go.

'I hope you will come to see us as frequently as you have always done. Wait; let me see what I shall give you as kola.'

'Mama, don't worry. You know I do not eat kola.'

Amadi's mother came out from her house with a small bag.

'Give these plums to your mother to roast for you. I don't have anything else in the house, as I have not been to market since Amadi left.'

Nwakaego left, fearing that the mention of Amadi's name would bring back memories that were better forgotten.

As she walked away, the eyes of Amadi's mother followed her. All this time her feelings about Amadi had been the feelings of a woman who was not sure whether she would ever set eyes on her son again; a woman whose son had gone to war. Here was a son who had raised everybody's hope, the pride of his parents, the boast of his mother, suddenly snatched away by wicked hands. And she, the mother who every other mother at Ezinkwo had envied, had suddenly become the topic for market gossip.

Now as she watched Nwakaego move away another unpleasant side of the situation opened out. Nwakaego too symbolised the major longing of every mother at Ezinkwo.

A wife for her son, a girl of her own choice, born of parents of her own choice and brought up in her own way. A daughter-in-law who would give her mother-in-law the respect she deserved. Above all, Nwakaego stood for the mother of her son's children, lively grandchildren on whom she would shower a grandmother's love and devotion. They were bound to be lively children, born by parents who had not wasted their youthful blood elsewhere.

She could feel these dreams, these hopes, dangle alluringly in front of her, and then vanish from her reach as Nwakaego took the bend and disappeared from her sight. Amadi's father came back from the farm to find her sobbing.

'What is wrong?' he asked. She made no reply, angry that she had again been caught weeping. She blew each nostril in turn, and wiped her eyes and nose with the loose end of her covering cloth.

'I hope you are not shedding tears still for what is over and done with.'

'I don't blame you. It is the person whose head is being shaved that feels the pain in the neck.'

'Do you think that you alone feel it? You think I am finding it as sweet as salt?'

'Why then do you keep your mouth like that when you talk to me?'

'Because the hymn book says that weeping cannot save anybody. What has happened has happened. Even if we shed enough tears to fill this room we cannot make yesterday tomorrow.'

'How do you know that anything has happened? How do you know that the story is true? What big lie has Amadi ever told us?'

'Now you are talking like a woman, so I had better leave you alone.'

He walked away from her and into his own house, to hang up his working clothes before having his usual warm bath. Her last remark brought back thoughts that had occupied his mind while he worked on the farm. But he had dismissed them as idle thoughts. He wished Amadi were innocent. The fear that such a wish might turn out to be without foundation made him dismiss it. It was better not to hope at all than to have false hope. As far as his mind could recall, no girl had been known to accuse the wrong man of being the father of her child, at least not in Ezinkwo.

18

'To think that I nearly committed suicide the day I set off from Onitsha to this place!'

Amadi was happy he had got the vacation job before he was rusticated; it made so much difference to him now. When he had applied for it, he had had no great hope of getting the job. Like many other undergraduates he simply wrote as many applications as possible: to schools, firms, corporations and Government departments all over the country, in the hope that at least one application would bring a favourable reply. The only offer he received came from a most unexpected source, the Grammar School at Uwhuvbe in the heart of Benin Province. He had no idea where the school was until he received the letter, and then he made detailed enquiries from some of the Beni students.

The atmosphere at Uwhuvbe made him forget his problems quickly. The town was off the flow of traffic. No one in the neighbourhood knew him, so there was no one to ask him embarrassing questions. His teaching load was very heavy as the school wanted to make full use of him during the three months he stayed with them. Not only was he required to brush up the School Certificate class in History, but he also had to teach English, Latin and Mathematics to other classes. The Student Christian Movement in the School expected him to give leadership to their branch, and other Societies too approached him for help. In the evenings he was kept busy on the games field. It was only on Sunday evenings that he had some time to himself, but even this was soon taken up when the girls teaching in a nearby convent discovered that he was good at ballroom dancing. They held their dancing practices in the house of the Headmistress who owned a gramophone and some records. It was a pleasant exercise for Amadi, although he made every effort to avoid being emotionally entangled with any of the girls. One of them appealed very strongly to him, but he refused to encourage his feelings. His entanglement with Sweetie, Aduke and Nwakaego gave him more headache than he could cope with; to add another girl would be suicidal. Moreover, he felt certain that the Headmistress would resent any association between him and one of her junior teachers, and there is no limit to what a jealous woman can do.

His vacation at Uwhuvbe gave him the opportunity to examine his predicament with a cool head.

He remembered that ominous day when he took Sweetie from the Zoo to his room. What a difference it would have made if he had not met her that afternoon. If only he had listened to Aduke and joined the Student Christian Movement group that had gone on a retreat that week-end, he would not have been rusticated by the University and rejected by his parents.

Perhaps this was the hand of God. Otherwise why should he have refused to take part in the retreat? Why should he accidentally have met Sweetie that afternoon? Now the idea of her conception appeared an act of Providence. He remembered every detail of the affair. Sweetie had made it abundantly clear to him that he was very welcome to have sex with her. He did no' wish to accept the offer for fear of catching one of the many diseases he had heard Lagos girls often hawk, and for fear of having an unwanted baby. But the sight of a charming girl dressed only in a pair of earrings was a bit too much for him, and when, in addition, Sweetie decided to try some sex play, his resistance broke down completely. It was his first attempt to make love with any girl, and it had happened exactly as he had told the Academic Registrar. A disappointed and angry Sweetie had pushed him aside, calling him names. He had apologised profusely and felt ashamed about his incompetence, but later he rejoiced that things had ended that way. He could not have caught any disease, neither could there be any danger of an unwanted baby. When, some weeks later, Sweetie wrote to report that she had missed her time, he decided to ignore the letter completely, as he was convinced that what had transpired between them was not sufficient to give a girl a baby, more especially a girl who claimed to be a virgin.

He was compelled to change his attitude when he went to see the Medical Officer in Benin. He was shocked to learn from the doctor that what had happened was enough for a girl to conceive, even if she were a virgin. The doctor had also warned him that he would have no defence in a law court. It now appeared he had no option but to write the note demanded by Sweetie and her mother. This would stop them from sending further reports to the University, and allow him to go back and complete his final year.

It was not easy to forget Nwakaego and Aduke. Even though he had begun to develop doubts about the wisdom of his engagement to Nwakaego during the previous long vacation, he still looked on her, immature though she was, as a perfect angel. He had not carried out his year-old resolution to write to his father, marshalling cogent arguments to explain why she was not a suitable match for him. His inner voice kept telling him that all he needed was a little patience and his reward would be an ideal wife. He knew her parents must be disappointed, but he felt certain she would find a good husband; girls like her never went husbandless. Perhaps a husband who would be a better match for her than he would. ' Nwakaego herself could not have had any deep emotional feelings for me. I am sure she has merely been carrying out her parents' instructions,' he thought.

Aduke was the girl who had dazzled him in the University; although when he was first drawn to her he had had no designs about marriage. The idea of making love to a University student was a novelty, and the fact that she was Yoruba made the adventure even more exciting. He wanted to prove to himself that he could break fresh ground. He also secretly hoped to make history as the first Ibo undergraduate to conquer a Yoruba girl in the University. Marriage was out of it. He knew his parents would never hear of such a match, even if Nwakaego had not existed, and he was sure Aduke's parents would not contemplate betrothing their daughter to an uncivilised ' Kobokobo ' from an unmapped part of Eastern Nigeria.

His interest in Aduke grew daily. She was an attractive girl, a fact that had been acknowledged even by Chima. She was his intellectual equal and did not exasperate him in the way Nwakaego sometimes did. She had chosen him as her University friend in preference to all the Yoruba men on the campus. From time to time he even found he was asking himself why Aduke should not make a good wife. She was temperamental, and her behaviour after he had told her about the Sweetie episode had been an even greater surprise to him. But who is perfect, he asked himself, especially in such circumstances? When the *Crocodile* cartoon appeared, he thought at first it might provide a good opportunity to test the strength of her feelings for him. Then the Sweetie incident upset the shaky scaffolding of hope he had been building up. He knew she did not believe his story. He tried to take offence at the thought that she did not trust him and rely on his words, but his conscience told him that he could lay no claim to such confidence. He had tried to have sexual intercourse with Sweetie, no matter how unsuccessful the attempt had turned out.

' God knows better than I,' he reasoned. ' From my youth, I have always felt that He has a plan for me. Who knows whether there is something in both Nwakaego and Aduke which I have not yet discovered, and which might have ruined my marriage to either of them? Who knows whether the Sweetie affair is not a blessing in disguise? '

He finally addressed the following letter to Sweetie:

Dear Sweetie,

I am sure you will be surprised to receive this letter, especially after my behaviour to you when you and your mother came to see me at the University.

I have now considered the matter very carefully, and I hereby declare my intention to marry you if the child you are now expecting is mine.

As it is against the custom of my people at Ezinkwo to negotiate marriage in respect of a girl expecting a baby, further negotiations will have to be suspended until after you have given birth. Best wishes

Amadi

19

Back at the University, Amadi retired from active life in the Students' Union. This was his final year, the year of reckoning. Practically all his mates had spent the last two months of the long vacation in residence, doing intensive reading, and he was aware that he would have to work longer than twenty-four hours a day if he was to catch up with them. Immediately after lectures each day he moved to the Library to work till lunch time. A brief siesta followed lunch, usually lasting about fifteen minutes and never exceeding half an hour. He then returned to the Library where he worked till 6.45 each evening and then hurried to his room to prepare for dinner. Immediately after the meal he went back to the Library, and remained there till it closed at ten o'clock. By that time the Hall was quiet and he could work in his room until after midnight when he went to bed. His Smith alarm, which he usually hung over the bed near his pillow, woke him at five o'clock in time for two hours' work before breakfast. He felt certain that if he worked regularly like this throughout the academic year he would walk away with a respectable degree. Chima had been able to do without even the siesta, yet he had not had a nervous breakdown. But Amadi did not want to take any chances, so he decided to leave the week-ends free, and from midday each Saturday he relaxed in whatever manner he thought fit. There was nothing he dreaded more than seeing a student being rushed to the Mental Hospital the day before his Finals.

His week-end relaxation often took the form of playing lawn tennis, watching matches either on the campus or in town, or visiting and chatting—anything that would take his mind off his studies. He was determined to keep women out of it. The words of the Professor of History came back to him from time to time: ' You can't get an A in History and an A in women.' Women could wait; the primary thing was the degree and, as the undergraduates often said, once you hold a degree all other good things will be added unto you.

The Improvement League had, after all, sent his full fees for the academic year. He had feared their reaction to his behaviour might lead them to withdraw their award and in anticipation of this he had dropped a hint to the Principal of the School at Uwhuvbe that he might have to apply to him for sponsorship. Unfortunately the year's sponsorship would have bound him to the school for two years after his graduation. Such a bond would have interfered with his ambition to become a District Officer. But now with his fees and allowances assured, and the small savings he had made at Uwhuvbe, he had everything he needed for a successful academic year.

He had not heard from his parents since that sorrowful morning he had left home, nor had he written. Thoughts about them came to him from time to time but he suppressed them. He had never in his life done anything that could have seriously displeased his parents. He had had a brilliant academic career so far and received good reports from School. He had always shown respect to his parents and elders, even when such signs of respect conflicted with his Western education; and even after going to the University he had done odd jobs at home—to the utter amazement of everybody at Ezinkwo. He could not therefore understand why he should be driven out of house and home because of his mishap with Sweetie. It pained him that his father would not accept his word. If his parents had decided to write him off for such an incident, he would accept their verdict. He would disappoint them if they expected him to assume the role of the repentant prodigal, returning home in rags to ask for forgiveness.

Amadi had just returned from morning service—a special service to raise funds for an enlarged Protestant Chapel. He picked up the programme of activities for the fund-raising week which was being organised by the Student Christian Movement. For want of something else to do he lay down, still in his Sunday clothes, to study the programme:

Monday, 26th Nov.: Manual work. S.C.M. members visit houses of Senior Staff, to do any work assigned to them, in return for money. ' I am too old for that, now,' he commented, and went on to the next day.

Tuesday, 27th Nov.: S.C.M. members visit Hospital to sing for the sick. ' I am sure croakers like me would be honourably excused! '

Wednesday, 28th Nov.: Football match, Women v. Men. ' That's great. I must watch that, even if only for part of the time.'

Thursday, 29th Nov.:

There was a knock on his door. His eyes moved from the programme to the door and he listened for a repeat performance, to make sure his ears were not deceiving him. Another knock.

' Yes! I'm coming.'

He turned the knob, opened the door and the Hall Porter walked in.

' Morning, Sir,' he saluted.

' Good morning, Porter. Anything? '

' No, Sir. I just wan' check whether master in.'

' Anybody asked about me? '

' Yes, Sir. One lady.'

' Where is she? ' asked Amadi anxiously, as if he suspected the Porter was deliberately keeping someone away from him.

' 'e don' go, Sir. Somebody say you no dey for Hall.'

' Nonsense,' Amadi retorted. ' Who said I was not in when I have been in all morning? '

' Na one student, Sir. 'e say 'e see de time you dey go away from Hall by ten o'clock.'

'So that means I must be away from the Hall all day. How did you know I was back now?'

'I no know, Sir. I jus' dey pass from room 58 and I say make I check should in case anoder person aks of you.'

'All right. Who was the girl?'

'She no tell me her name.'

'What a whole bunch of *makakwus* you Porters are!'

'Make master no curse me; O! I never curse master before.'

'I am not cursing you, my friend, but what's the point of telling me that someone looked for me when you would not bring her to my room, neither can you tell me her name.'

''e say 'e no go tell me her name because 'e go meet you for one *oyibo* man house tomorrow evening.'

'Tomorrow evening?'

'Yes, sir.'

'All right. Thank you. Next time a lady looks for me, bring her straight to my room.'

Amadi strolled along the corridor, stretching his neck in every possible direction in the vain hope that he might still catch a glimpse of the girl. Who could she be? Sweetie? Impossible; otherwise the porter could have described her as 'one pregnant woman'. In any case what would she be doing travelling when she was carrying an eight-month-old child. And if it had been her, she would have certainly insisted on waiting.

The reference to the meeting in a European's house the following day confused him further. He was not aware of an appointment with any European in the foreseeable future, He went to European houses only when he was invited. having formed the opinion that many Europeans were not sincere when they encouraged students to drop in on them without a formal invitation. He still remembered the rude way in which a European wife drove a group of them out of her husband's house when he was a Secondary schoolboy, simply because they had had the audacity to knock at the front door instead of calling first at the stewards' quarters behind the house to find out whether they were welcome.

His first clue came on Monday morning in the lecture room.

The Lecturer was late and the students filled in the time by ' gisting '. The topic was the Student Christian Movement and the discussion was led by one of the students who labelled the Movement the ' Student Chasing Movement ' and the ' Society for Courtship and Marriage '.

' The members are very clever,' remarked the leader. ' They use every activity of theirs to advantage.'

' Aren't you people tired of that stale joke? ' cut in Amadi. ' The S.C.M. is an open door Movement. Nothing prevents any of you from joining and getting the benefits you enumerate.'

' We don't need that kind of a Movement,' replied one of the opponents of the S.C.M. ' We know how to win girl friends by honest means. It is backboneless men—I mean no offence—who need your Movement to get girl friends.'

' Have you heard the latest? ' The leader was on his feet this time. ' Some of our good friends, whose names I shall leave out, have decided to pair up with the girls this evening. Each of them has been allowed to pick his girl friend or the girl he wishes to " drive ". And they say they are going to do God's work in the houses of Senior Staff. I suppose they would be doing the Devil's work if the men and the women worked in separate groups! '

His remarks were greeted with laughter, and many faces turned towards the few girls in the class.

Amadi did not feel like giving up. ' Trying to argue with some of you people is as fruitless as trying to carry a child with a fractured waist. When our girls keep to themselves you shout them down as being snobbish and unsociable. When they share every activity with their male counterparts you see some ulterior motives in their actions. I don't see anything wrong in what you criticise.'

' How could you? ' asked the leader. ' I refused to mention names to avoid embarrassing anybody. Don't compel me to say what I do not wish to say.'

' Please don't! ' shouted another student. ' Don't mention names. The people who tie cloth over their waists when bathing in a stream know themselves.'

The Lecturer walked in, apologising for his lateness which he said was due to a flat tyre, his usual excuse, and the lecture began.

When Amadi returned to his room after lunch, he found a note under his door. It was to inform him that he had been assigned to work for the Academic Registrar at five o'clock that evening. He crumpled the paper and flung it furiously into the waste-paper basket.

'I have no time to work for anybody, and certainly not for that double-faced Academic Registrar. If I fail my examination he certainly won't plead for me.'

Suddenly he remembered the message left by the unknown girl who had visited him. The message now had a meaning. From the way his classmates had pulled his leg, he must have been grouped with a girl to work for a member of the Senior Staff and the girl who called must have been his work companion, and, of course, the Academic Registrar was the European.

Which girl could it be? For some reason he could not explain, he hoped it would be Aduke, while at the same time fearing that he might be proved right.

'Well! Perhaps I should go. One hour off my work can't hurt. And it's an hour spent in His service.'

As he lay on his bed that night, scanning the S.C.M. programme for the rest of the week, he wondered whether his decision to work that afternoon had been wise.

The first embarrassment came when the Academic Registrar recognised him.

'Your face looks like a face I have seen more than once,' he said, shaking hands with Amadi. 'I must apologise, I'm no good at remembering names. And Nigerian names present a special difficulty to non-Nigerians; they all seem so impossible to pronounce.'

Amadi refused to say his name. He hoped the Academic Registrar would read from his face that he was in no mood for friendly exchanges.

The Academic Registrar went on. 'Now let me think. I think I've got it. Forgive me if I've made a mistake, but weren't you the student reported to me for giving a girl a baby and refusing to accept the responsibility?'

'I have now sent her the note you ordered me to give her,' replied Amadi.

'Brave lad!' and he patted Amadi on the shoulder. 'That's the spirit. Nothing to fear about marriage. It's as easy to contract out of as it is to contract in!' He chuckled as he walked away.

Aduke who was present during this exchange, said nothing; she gave the impression that she was not listening to what the two were discussing.

Amadi broke the uncomfortable silence which followed the departure of the Academic Registrar.

'Aduke, isn't it surprising that you have not bothered to find out what has happened to me? I suppose it would have meant nothing to you if I had been sent down for good.'

'Yes.'

'Aduke, you are saying that?'

'Well, when you asked me the question what reply did you expect?'

'I am very sorry. It was stupid of me to have asked the question. I was encouraged to do so because you called at my room yesterday to see me. I thought you had something to discuss with me.'

'Yes, but we've come here to work. I may have something to say when the work's finished.'

Amadi could not remember afterwards how they found themselves sitting shoulder to shoulder on one of the improvised benches in the University Park.

'Amadi, I am deeply sorry for everything.'

'About what?' asked Amadi.

'About my behaviour. I'm sorry that it was one of the few occasions when I seemed to lose control over my feelings. I'm sure it won't happen again. I'm also sorry for not believing your story.'

'But nobody believed me. The University authorities didn't believe me, and so I was rusticated. Even my own parents, who have never had cause to doubt me, wouldn't believe me. I haven't told you but they sent me packing from home for bringing such unheard-of disgrace to the family. So *you've* no cause to apologise for not believing my story.'

'Do you mean your parents took such a firm stand? Was it because Sweetie was not Ibo?'

'Not exactly. My parents are leading members of the village Church. They therefore frown at the idea of pre-marital babies. To them I had committed a great sin and smeared them with mud. Any Ezinkwo man involved like this is usually expected to marry the expectant mother; there is no such thing as criminal abortion. So they expected me to marry Sweetie, and the thought of it has nearly sent my father crazy. The thought that his first son would bring an unknown prostitute into his house to become his daughter-in-law, the realisation that he had for many years toiled to crack kernels which were now falling for the chickens; it was more than he could swallow and so he showed me the door.'

'Would he have done the same if Sweetie had been a native of your village?'

'He would have felt hurt and disgraced. Whether he would have shown me the door would have depended on the kind of girl she was.'

Aduke did not say anything, so Amadi went on.

'Anyway, I've taken a final decision on the matter.'

'What is it?'

'What you heard me tell the Academic Registrar a short while ago.'

'Are you serious?'

'Yes.'

'Why?'

'Because I ought to take full responsibility for my irre-sponsibility.'

'That is if you *are* responsible for the baby. How can she prove that you are? Those Lagos girls pass from one bed to another. How is she sure that it was you and not another man who gave her the baby?'

'Sweetie said she was a virgin when she came to my room.

If she became pregnant after leaving me, who else could have been responsible? '

' Virgin indeed! What Lagos girl is a virgin? Not even the schoolgirls.'

' Aduke, I only wish you had argued like this some months ago.'

Aduke turned slightly away from him. ' You're talking like a man. Put yourself in my position and see whether you would have reacted differently.'

' I don't understand.'

' You never do. Both of us have been friends for some time. At least, we've got on well together even if we have not been close friends. You don't know how much I've suffered because of my connection with you, from my people and from my fellow students. And all the time you gave me the impression that all your cards were face up. The attack in the *Crocodile* was the first sign that I was being unrealistic. But I was prepared to ignore it. Then came a Lagos street girl. First of all, you didn't want me to know that she and her mother had come to extract a promise of marriage from you. You didn't want me to know they were in your room that afternoon you were so rude to me. In spite of all this, you expected me to believe your story before you had even told it. You expected me to be cool-headed and logical when I heard that you'd taken another girl to bed.'

Amadi could not believe his ears. His urge was to hug her, but he feared he might be repelled. He leaned back on the wooden bench and drew her gently so that her head rested on his chest. When he noticed that she did not object, he gently lifted her up on to his lap.

' Please give me my handbag.'

Amadi noticed an unsteadiness in her voice. She took out her handkerchief, dabbed her eyes and blew her nose.

' Aduke, please don't do that or you will upset me.'

' You can be upset if you like. Does it matter to you how much you've upset me? Does it matter to you how much weight I've lost in the last months? Does it matter to you that I've become the laughing stock of many of my friends who had warned me right from the start not to become emotionally involved with an Ibo man, because he would use me as a stop-gap and abandon me later to marry a girl reserved for him in his village? Does it . . .'

' It's enough, Aduke. You've said more than enough if that's what you think of me. Have you ever asked yourself how much I've had to suffer for your sake? '

' What have you suffered? '

' I feel it's childish to begin to say what I've suffered or to proclaim my feelings towards you. He who knows our innermost thoughts knows how I'd made up my mind not to marry Nwakaego, the pretty girl who was betrothed to me as soon as she was born, and on whose head my parents have spent so much money. He alone knows how much love I've nursed for you, and how I've feared to give expression to it, being uncertain what your reaction would be, coming as you do from a different tribe. He alone knows why I've taken the decision I've taken.'

' What decision? ' There was optimism in her eyes as she looked at him.

' The one I've already told you. To marry Sweetie.'

' Do you seriously mean that you're going to marry that girl? '

' What d'you expect me to do? This is the first time, since we became friends, that you have shown me that you would have me as a husband.'

' Did you ever ask me? Or do women, in your place, propose to men? '

' It's true I didn't. But how could I? Each time I spoke of inter-tribal marriages you ran through a long list of the problems which would make such marriages unsuccessful— language difficulties, the long distance between your home and mine, cultural differences, political problems, and so on. D'you remember once telling me that your grandmother threatened to die if you married a ' Kobokobo '. To crown it all, the Sweetie affair dropped from nowhere. Nobody was prepared to believe my story, not even you. I thought every-thing over during my stay at Uwhuvbe and I decided that the only honourable thing to do was to marry Sweetie.'

' Have you told her so? '

'I am afraid I have. I wrote to her during the vac and I don't see how I can get out of it now.'

'Let's go,' was all Aduke said. They did not speak to each other on their way back, except when Aduke told him he need not accompany her to her Hall.

20

'Had I known! Had I but known . . .' Amadi spent the rest of his reading time that night imagining what would have happened if only he had known that Aduke was prepared to marry him, even in the teeth of opposition from all sides. He felt he had had a raw deal, the way a man feels cheated who in his dream has conquered a 'mammy water'. The stage is set, the comely 'mammy water' is willing to give him the greatest thrill of his life; she places herself at his disposal and nothing more separates him from the dish that every mortal man would relish. As he plants his knees on both sides of her, a cock crows and drags him back to reality. Much as he shuts his eyes tight after that, sleep fails to come, when it does come the 'mammy water' has returned to the depths of the ocean, far from mortal reach.

That was how Amadi felt. But he need not blame himself. He had done all he could in the time available. He would have had to get rid of Nwakaego before proposing to Aduke, and this he had tried to do, but then came the Sweetie affair with its unpredicted consequences—on the one hand snapping the ties with Nwakaego and on the other alienating him from Aduke. To declare for Sweetie seemed the inevitable consequence, and he had done so.

'Pity Chima has left the University. His down-to-earth intelligence might have come in handy.'

It was painful to take his mind off Aduke. If he had lost her and won a girl of his tribe, acceptable to his parents, the position might have been tolerable. But by marrying Sweetie, he was marrying outside his tribe, something which was objectionable to his parents; worse still, he was marrying a girl of doubtful character whom he would not have married had he not given her a baby. And for this his parents had disowned him. Not only had he eaten a toad, but he had chosen to eat a scraggy one!

'There's one thing I'm not so sure about, though,' he pondered. 'Would Aduke have come out so openly if Sweetie had not appeared on the scene? Is she professing deep interest in me out of sheer jealousy or because she knows there is no future in the game? Pity there is no way in which I can check this. But there is! I could tell her that I have decided to renounce Sweetie and to marry her. But suppose she says yes, how can I withdraw my promissory letter to Sweetie? I shall only be giving her a chance to damage my name further, and this time it might mean dismissal, not rustication. And if I know Aduke, a decision to renounce Sweetie may only belittle me in her eyes without winning me her hand. And then I would be a complete bat, alienated from the right and from the left.'

Graduation Day celebrations were the main event of the term. They conformed to the usual pattern—the colourful academic procession, the conferment of degrees, the colourless 'spectatorless' cricket match between Senior Staff and students, the Vice-Chancellor's cocktail party to which the only students invited were members of the Students' Representative Council. The day usually ended with the Graduation-day Ball which was never known to be crowded, especially as it was organised mainly by Lecturers; this time the attendance was even poorer than usual.

Amadi was fortunate to get a card for the gallery, and he watched the degree ceremony with particular interest. This was his last year as an undergraduate, and if things went well, by this time next year it would be his turn to receive a degree certificate. The ceremony was solemn. The University Registrar requested the Dean of each Faculty to present the men and women in his faculty who 'in character and learning' had been considered suitable for degree awards.

As the Dean read each name, the incepting graduate was marshalled to the foot of the steps where the appropriate hood was put on him. He then walked up the steps to the Chancellor who held him by the hand and pronounced the formula of inception: 'By the authority vested on me I hereby receive you as a graduate member of this University, holding the degree of Bachelor of . . .' Amid applause from the audience, which usually diminished in intensity after the first few names, except when it was the turn of a girl or a controversial or well known member of the Students' Union, the new graduate moved down the steps to the table where he was handed a piece of paper, looking very much like blotting paper. This was the symbol of success, the 'golden fleece' in quest of which Nigerians had previously travelled far and wide. Now it was available in their own country.

Amadi was surprised to hear Chima's name called. At first he thought it must be a mistake. Chima had not written to him since leaving the University in June. Even the congratulatory telegram Amadi sent him when the degree results were published in August had not been acknowledged. At first Amadi thought he might show up at the degree ceremony' but as he had received no letter from him to that effect, he concluded that Chima probably found it inconvenient to come. He would be among those whose degrees would be received by proxy by their Dean because 'for grave cause they could not be present.

'That's Chima for sure,' muttered Amadi, as Chima moved to the steps. He clapped his loudest as Chima descended the steps to receive his degree certificate.

Immediately after the ceremony he made a frantic search for him.

'Hello, man. Hearty congratulations!' They shook hands very warmly.

'This na your eye?' asked Amadi.

'Well, eye and its companion, if I may follow your language.'

'Did you get my telegram?'

'Yes, thank you. I'm sorry I just couldn't make the time to acknowledge it.'

'In which Department are you working?' asked Amadi.

'I am the Assistant D.O. at Amagu.'

'What? I can't believe it. Do you mean you are looking after my District? That's great! I wonder whether you've paid a visit to Ezinkwo?'

'I do a lot of touring,' replied Chima evasively. 'I'm afraid I can't remember now all the villages I have covered.'

'Why didn't you write to tell me you were coming? I could easily have vacated my room for you.'

'Well—I suppose I should have written. But I am a busy man. Also, I thought it wouldn't be fair.'

'Don't be funny! Does the Senior Service transform someone into an Englishman overnight? Not fair indeed for me to vacate my room for a friend! Tell me something else.'

'Well, I thought that in present circumstances it wouldn't be expedient.'

'What circumstances?' asked Amadi, baffled.

'I'll tell you before I go. It's not the sort of thing one discusses in this kind of place. Moreover, some people are waiting to be photographed with me and I must get through all that before lunch time.'

'Where are you putting up? On the campus or in town?'

'I'm around generally, to use an undergraduate expression. Never mind, I'll do my best to see you before I go. 'Bye for now.'

Amadi was shocked. That was not the Chima he had known only a few months ago. What could have changed him overnight? Could it have anything to do with his new job? District and Assistant District Officers were often treated as little short of gods in villages like Ezinkwo, and they were usually swollen-headed as a result. But Chima did not need to be reminded that he was now at the University campus, where he was an insignificant quantity, and not at Ezinkwo where the simple folk would be surprised to see the A.D.O. urinate or drink palm wine. He should also know that Amadi was only a year behind him.

Or could his behaviour have been caused by the fact that Amadi came from Ezinkwo? Was he afraid to associate openly with a 'son of the soil'?

None of these reasons seemed convincing enough to Amadi as he walked slowly back to his Hall. At the gate the Porter handed him a letter.

'That looks like Chima's writing. Well, he did take the trouble to look me up. That's better. I couldn't believe he could forget me so quickly.'

He tore open the envelope. 'But why couldn't he have told me that he'd called here instead of taking up that strange kind of attitude?'

He stood by the bicycle park and with anxious fingers unfolded the letter.

Dear Mr Chukwuka,
I seem to have a tight schedule for my brief visit and it is possible I may not see you before I return to my station. I have therefore decided to drop you these few lines.
In a month or two from now I should be formally engaged to Miss Nwakaego Ikwvaju. She comes from Ezinkwo, although I am not sure whether you know her.
My very best wishes as the day of reckoning draws near.
Yours, etc.

Amadi read the letter over and over again. That explains it; that explains it. I knew there was something fishy. Chima is not the man to behave like an Englishman for nothing. He knew he had hit me below the belt. He knows my connection with Nwakaego; after all, haven't I always gone to him for advice? To give the impression he was not sure if I knew her was a very cheap thing to do.

He walked to his room, lay down and read the letter twice over before folding it and putting it back into the envelope. He searched the drawers of his table and produced a photograph of Nwakaego. It was the only photograph of her in his possession, and it had once occupied a privileged position on the top of his book shelf. It was the photograph that had given rise to the *Crocodile* attack. Chima had always shown great admiration for the girl in the photograph. He talked of her as ' an example of the innocent beauties we have in the East ' as opposed to the ' superficial old-timers in Oliaku Hall who need University education to enhance their chances of getting husbands'.

He held the photograph close to his eyes, and surveyed Nwakaego from head to foot—her bright eyes, her innocent smile, her superb form. Nwakaego was beautiful, naturally beautiful, beautiful without the help of make-up. She was innocent, the kind of girl who went to her husband's house intact. She had been brought up in a home where the wife accepted the authority of her husband and the husband knew the woman's role. She came from his village, spoke not only the same language but also the same dialect as he spoke. She was acceptable to his parents who had longed to call her their daughter-in-law. Yet he had been reluctant to marry her. Why? Because she was not sufficiently educated? Because she was not a University graduate? Because she was not fit to become the wife of a District Officer, precisely what Chima would soon make her? Aduke had dazzled him so much that he had become blind to Nwakaego's good points. What an idiot he had been! And what a price he was paying for his blindness, his stupidity!

He kissed Nwakaego's smiling lips, pressed the photograph to his chest and extended it for another glance.

' Nwakaego, I owe you every apology. I'm sorry for the shabby treatment I gave you. But I'm prepared to make amends. I'm prepared to put this in writing right now if it will make any difference.'

The door opened and Aduke walked in.

' I thought I heard a voice in here. I gave one or two knocks, got no reply, and, as I didn't want to stand out there all day, I turned the key and came in. To whom were you talking? '

' Look in the wardrobe,' replied Amadi.

As Aduke walked towards the wardrobe he tried to hide Nwakaego's photograph in his shirt pocket, forgetting that the shirt had no pocket. The photograph dropped to the floor. Aduke turned sharply and saw him picking it up.

' What are you up to? ' she asked. ' Is that your future wife's photograph or have you made a new catch? '

'Yes,' replied Amadi, handing the photograph to her. 'And what do you think of my taste?'

Aduke scrutinised the photograph for some time before she spoke. 'I'm sure I have seen this photograph before.'

'You sure have. This was the wife I was accused of keeping at home while making useless love to you. This was the photograph that provoked the attack in the *Crocodile*. You couldn't have come at a better time. Read this letter from my friend Chima and judge whether or not I was playing fair with you.'

Aduke read the letter and gave it back to Amadi. 'I'm sorry if I have unwittingly hurt you in any way, Amadi. But I thought the matter was now closed. We've accepted the inevitable, haven't we? I've come here for something else. Will you come to the dance tonight?'

'Well, that's a difficult one. I had really made up my mind not to go. But if you feel like going, I suppose I could change my mind.'

'You don't have to if you don't want to. Dotun Kolawole has been pestering me to go with him, he wants me to celebrate his graduation. To put him off I told him that I'd promised to go with you. If I don't, well, I don't know how it will look.'

'Oh, I see. Well, I'll go with you, even though this doesn't seem the most discreet moment to attend dances together.'

'Little men have little minds. In any case, what more can they say about us? You're as good as married now, so it couldn't look as if I was begging you to marry me or vice versa. After my talk with you in the University Park I thought matters over. I thought I shouldn't have behaved the way I did. You did the right thing by deciding to marry Sweetie. If I'd been in her shoes I would have expected nothing short of that from you. So I've also come to apologise. The fact that we can't become husband and wife shouldn't prevent us from remaining innocent Christian friends just as we have always been.'

'Aduke, you are simply too good for me, and I don't want to say more than that. Perhaps it's God's desire that we should remain nothing but friends. He sees beyond the reach of human eyes. I'll call at your Hall to take you to the dance. What time suits you? '

'I'll be ready at ten o'clock.'

21

The Christmas term ended on the 13th of December. According to University custom, only the final year students were allowed to remain in residence during the vacation and make use of the library and laboratories. The other students had to leave the campus in order to make room for the many vacation conferences normally organised by the Extramural Department of the University. The University authorities also argued that it was in the interest of the students to give their brains an occasional holiday.

Amadi had an even stronger case for remaining in residence than the other final year students. He had been rusticated shortly before the end of the previous term. In addition to this, he had not returned to residence during the months of August and September when all his classmates had been allowed to return to the campus to read. Even though he had done some reading at the school where he had done his vacation teaching, he felt the students who returned to the campus had done infinitely more work than he had. They must have consumed the contents of all the historical journals and reserved books. His fears were heightened by the fact that not one of the students he had approached would show him the ground they had covered during these two months. Almost all of them complained that they had loafed away the two months, although one of them infuriated him by saying that he had been thinking of consulting Amadi, because he heard from reliable sources that Amadi had hibernated during the four months of the long vacation and had done nothing but swot.

In spite of his setbacks, Amadi had had a successful term, so the Professor told him at the end-of-term interview.

'Mr Chukwuka,' began the Professor, ' I was a bit worried about you at the beginning of term, especially as we didn't have the opportunity of testing you at the end of last session. You have done good work this term. If you keep up your present pace, you ought to make a good second comfortably.'

Amadi was a happy man. The Professor was never known to tell any student that he was first class material. The first class was said to be reserved for angels; the best students in every set of finalists were always said to have ' missed a first very narrowly '. To be told by the Professor that one would get a good second was a sure sign that the student would graduate.

' By the way,' the Professor went on, ' what has become of that girl who brought about your rustication last term? '

' She is in Lagos.'

' Have you ironed out your differences? '

' Up to a point, Sir. Somehow, I feel that I am innocent. But the University authorities would not accept my word. In the circumstances, I had no alternative but to promise to marry the girl, against my conscience and the wishes of my parents.'

' Perhaps we needn't go into all that in detail.' The Professor was becoming shifty. ' I am sure you appreciate why I raised the matter. You appear to be among our better students, and I am anxious to ensure that domestic problems don't interfere with your work. That's all for now. Ask the next student to come in.'

Three students waiting for their turn surrounded Amadi. ' How was it? ' they asked. ' You took such a long time.'

' Nothing in particular,' Amadi replied. ' The Professor was only warning me about the ground I lost last term.'

The men left him to await their turn.

Thoughts of Sweetie haunted Amadi for the rest of the day. Much as he had tried he could not get her out of his mind, especially at this time. Judging by the account she gave when she reported him to the University authorities, the baby should be due any moment.

'So shall I soon be a father?' he asked himself. He swelled with pride at the thought. It was a mark of achievement, proof that he had some power between his thighs. He knew some men who were incapable of giving a woman a child, whose semen was mere water. There was a well-known example at Ezinkwo, not only was he impotent, but it was also believed that if he went to bed with a pregnant woman she would automatically miscarry.

His feeling of elation was counteracted by other less pleasant thoughts. How was he to be sure that the child was his? How could union of that kind produce a child when married men often spent months of active nights with their wives before achieving success? Yet the doctor had said it was possible. So the child could be his.

He had often consoled himself with the hope that the baby itself would give the verdict. If the child resembled him, there could be no further doubt. But suppose the child resembled Sweetie? That would be useless evidence.

Assuming the child turned out to be his, was he ready for a family of his own? He was still only an undergraduate, with no means of income. To make matters worse, his parents had cast him off like a tattered dress. He would not want his first child to suffer undue hardship or to be brought up in squalor. In his glorious moments before all this happened he had pictured his children being pushed along in grand perambulators, with innumerable toys to play with and with a nurse-girl in immaculate white to minister to their needs. But perhaps it would not be too bad. The child would only suffer for a few months—with a degree in his pocket he was still guaranteed the good things of life. A car, a refrigerator, and the rest . . .

One other thought bothered him and that was whether the child would be a boy or a girl. To rear a family of girls was the worst fate that could befall any couple at Ezinkwo. A woman who produced only girls knew that her tenure was very insecure. Sooner or later her husband's relations would advise him to look for a woman who could give him a son.

A man who died without male issue was lost to posterity. His *obi* would revert to the bush soon after his death, and his name would forever be forgotten because there was no son to perpetuate it. To begin the family with a son was a guarantee that the man's name would not be lost. Amadi hoped he would get a son. If his prayers were answered he would name him Chukwuma, which means ' God knows ': God alone would know whether the child was his or another man's.

The birth of a son was the one hope of reconciliation with his parents. A daughter would not be a good enough treasure to lay at their feet, but a son could hardly be resisted.

' I must go down to Lagos to find out what is happening. I don't think I can wait until I hear from Sweetie.'

At first he thought of spending Christmas in Lagos. Later he decided he should wait till the last week of the vacation. Surely the child would have arrived by then and his trip would not be wasted—the time spent out of the campus would give his brain a short but welcome rest before the second term began.

22

As Amadi and Aduke passed patches of flowers in the University Park, Aduke began to ask why on earth she had agreed to pay another visit to the Park in his company.

' You're always full of whys and wherefores,' remarked Amadi, trying to reassure her. ' We can't spend eternity on earth. Why not relax while we can and make the best use of our short stay here? '

' Nobody says you mustn't enjoy yourself while you can, but must you always enjoy it with Aduke in the University Park? '

' I'm sorry for tying a rope round your neck and dragging

you down here.' Amadi had a mischievous smile on his lips.
'In any case, how many times have we come down here
together?'

'Once, but that one experience is not worth repeating.
I agreed to come then because there was still a link
between us.'

'Now be consistent, Aduke. Have you forgotten what you
told me that night you came to ask me to take you to the
Graduation-day Ball? It isn't two months ago.'

'Being seen together at a dance is different from being
seen loitering at this hour in the shady patches of the Park.'

'Of course, I know. The difference is that down here
anything could happen.'

'Really?' Aduke smiled cynically. 'Why are you wasting
time then?'

'Don't rush me. I have my plans.' As he said so, he
gently picked up her left hand and gave it a squeeze. She
quickly pushed him aside.

'You had better keep your distance if your plans have
begun to hatch.'

They moved on in silence.

'Aduke! All jokes aside, I have something to discuss with
you.'

'So you told me outside the library when you diverted me
here. I have been waiting hungrily for it.'

'But it's not something I can discuss when you're in such
an aggressive mood. It's a heart-to-heart talk, and we need
to settle down on the seat beneath that good old umbrella
tree.'

'Provided you remember you are a married man.'

'Not yet,' Amadi cut in.

'Married or not yet married, it's all the same to me. You
have given your word to Sweetie and a Christian's word is
his bond. So make sure you don't try any experiments
with me.'

'Bravo, my chief of the Student Christian Movement!
You speak as if you were reading from the Scriptures.'

'If that's what you planned to discuss with me, perhaps
we'd better be going.'

They moved slowly towards the umbrella tree. Amadi quickly dusted the log seat with his handkerchief and signalled Aduke to sit. She hesitated for a while and then sat down. Amadi squeezed in by her side.

' Aduke, you remember the last time we were here together.'

Aduke interrupted. ' You mean the only time we have been here together. Don't talk as if we lived in the University Park. The only other time I came here with you was in the company of your Old Boys.'

' It doesn't matter to me which way you put it. The only time we were here together—I hope that gladdens your heart —we discussed delicate issues.'

' Like your announcement to me that you were as good as married to Sweetie and therefore I must know my bounds. That was indeed a delicate issue.'

' Aduke, can't you give me a hearing? '

' I suppose I have to, especially as there's no cotton wool in my ears.'

' As I was saying before I was rudely interrupted,' continued Amadi, ' the last time—sorry, the only time we were here together—you thought I had been insincere with you. If I remember your expression, you thought I did not place all my cards on the table.'

He paused a little. Aduke's face showed signs of impatience.

' I want to ask you a silly question. Please give me a frank answer. Suppose Sweetie had not appeared on the scene at all, would you have accepted a proposal from me? '

' And what is the purpose of this big exercise? '

' Your answer is of tremendous importance to me.'

' I know it is. Not only will it boost your ego if I say yes, confirming your assessment of yourself as the boy that girls run around, but it would also give you something to discuss with your friends. " You know what, that girl is head over heels in love with me. She told me in no unmistaken terms that she would do anything for me if only I promised to marry her." Wouldn't that sound grand? '

"Aduke, I hope you will not hurt me deliberately. Surely you know me better than that.'

'I'm sorry. But I still don't know why this question arises.'

'If it didn't mean much to me as well as to you, I wouldn't be asking it. You can answer it or leave it.'

'*Rora, O!* Don't blow me up, O!'

Amadi appeared angry and disappointed. 'I don't blow people up. I keep no explosives.'

'O.K., let's forget it. Your question is embarrassing. I'm sure you know how I feel about you, and there's hardly anything I can add to it.'

'Yes, I know how you feel about me,' echoed Amadi. 'But I also know that you've often talked about all the practical difficulties. That's why I'm wondering whether you were serious when you made me understand that you would've agreed to marry me, if I hadn't been involved with Sweetie.'

'Amadi, if you ask students who know me well, they'll tell you that I'm often brief with men. It may be because of the way I was brought up, it may be because I'm still comparatively young. You yourself know how few other men I've moved around with on this campus the way I've moved around with you, even if you count the students from my home town. And you know how long it took me to decide to associate with you. It's true we come from different parts of the country—as a matter of fact, I am not sure I can locate your village on a map of Nigeria, neither can I pronounce the name easily. All the same, there are some qualities I've found in you which I've not found in the few men who have come my way—qualities which I am sure could have made me forget our tribal differences. Moreover, Achebe's *Things Fall Apart* showed me that these differences are not as great as I'd imagined. But this is now useless talk.'

Amadi produced an envelope from the pocket of his trousers opened it carefully, spread out the paper inside and handed it to Aduke.

'I hope it isn't too dark for you to read this.'

Aduke's heart throbbed against her ribs as she took a quick glance through the letter in her hands. It was addressed the Vice-Chancellor of the University.

Dear Sir,

I am compelled in fairness to Mr A. Chukwuka, one of your undergraduates, to confess that the report I made for you about him which led to his rustication last academic year is false. Now that I have given birth to the baby I was expecting, I feel convinced that he was not responsible for my pregnancy. My mother and I have accordingly withdrawn our request that he should marry me, and we apologise for all the trouble we gave you in this matter.

Yours faithfully,

Sweetie M. Akpore

Aduke read it a second time before she flashed an enquiring glance at Amadi. Amadi, who had been watching her all the time, smiled broadly at her.

' How come? ' was all she could ask. Then, after a slight pause, she continued: ' This sounds very much like you.'

' I didn't know you had mastered my style,' replied Amadi, pleased that she could recognise his language so easily. ' Well, to tell you the truth, I drafted the letter and asked her to copy it out and sign it.'

' Under duress? '

' That wasn't necessary. The letter was all I demanded of her and her mother, and they were only too pleased to give it. They feared I would make more difficult demands, or that I might even take them to court for damaging my name.'

' Come on, don't keep me in suspense indefinitely. What's all this mean? '

' It all means that you should have trusted your friend. Sweetie has given birth and the child is not mine. She gave birth about a month ago, but because she knew she had accused me falsely she didn't want to notify me about the arrival of the baby.'

' But how could you prove so easily that the child wasn't yours? '

' The fact was obvious to any one who had eyes to see. The child is a mulatto and everyone in Lagos knows its father—a white Permanent Secretary in the Ministry of Production.'

'Amadi, this is one of the greatest surprises of my life, and I hardly know what to say. I'm thoroughly ashamed of myself. I should have known better and I hope you'll forgive me.'

'I shall forgive you and forget all about it, provided you accept a late New Year's present from me.'

'I don't like conditions. May I see the present first?'

'Lack of trust again?'

'Oh, Amadi, don't be impossible! Give me whatever the present is. I accept it.'

'I hid it over there,' said Amadi, pointing to another part of the Park. 'Could we go there and fetch it?'

Aduke was full of expectation as they moved off. Unobtrusively, Amadi picked up her left hand and began to slip something on to her third finger. Conscious that something odd was happening to her finger, she glanced at it, wondering what trick Amadi could be playing. What she saw was beyond her.

Amadi!'

'Yes, darling. That's the New Year's present which you have accepted. If you hold on a minute, I shall try to put it on properly. The owner of the jewellery shop where I bought it said that if it didn't fit we could go back and select the proper size.'

Aduke examined her finger and the three-stone ring on it. Without thinking she threw her arms round Amadi and clung to him like a tick. Amadi balanced himself firmly to receive her. He pressed her so hard that he feared he might squeeze the life out of her. The experience was stimulating to both of them, and Aduke did not know when he carried her back to their old seat.

Amadi could hear himself breathe. Aduke's eyes were closed and she seemed to have left herself completely at his disposal. He attempted to kiss her but it was only a meeting of two pairs of lips. When he sucked she did not reciprocate. He quietly undid one of the buttons of her blouse and slipped in his hand. What it encountered were round and warm.

He desisted from squeezing them for fear that he might hurt her, he simply moved his hand from one to the other, thrilled by their velvet smoothness. Aduke came to herself with a start, which made him withdraw his hand as if he had been caught stealing meat from the soup pot.

' I think we've gone far enough,' she observed.

' Have we? ' Amadi replied, for want of something better to say. He was thoroughly excited and, like most men, would have liked to go further.

' We mustn't begin foolishly,' she continued, ' or we might end up the Sweetie way.'

' O.K. But I hope you've enjoyed the experience so far.'

' Of course I have. This is the first time I'm having such an experience in my life. I'm happy it was with a reasonable man like you, otherwise I might have had more than I bargained for. Don't you think we'd better be going? '

She took his arm.

' Give me a little moment,' he replied, smiling. ' I need to cool off a little before we move, otherwise everybody who passes us on the way will draw conclusions.'

' As if I care! Those jobless boys can now gossip as much as they wish. You are mine and I am yours, and that's all that matters.'

As they walked back to Oliaku Hall, Amadi noticed the change of attitude in Aduke. She no longer objected if he held her hand, and her happiness was clearly written on her face. He too was a very happy man. For the first time in his life he had made a conquest. And what a conquest! He was pleased too that she was the responsive type. He had been warned by friends to avoid the unresponsive girl. A member of his Hall had narrated the experience he had when he visited a girl friend during the long vacation. The girl was busy writing her notes of lessons for the following week, oblivious of the fact that the boy was playing with her nipples in a futile effort to work her up. He might just as well have been playing with the nipples on an ebony carving!

Aduke was responsive. That was probably why she kept men at a distance. To be responsive was a pleasant quality in a girl provided she did not fall into wrong hands. But

Aduke was not the type to fall into wrong hands. He believed her when she said it was her first experience, the way she kissed was ample evidence of that.

I shall teach her to kiss, he resolved secretly. She must learn to suck like the girl Mr Okoye nicknamed the Little Cannibal, and to play with her tongue between my teeth in Sweetie's intriguing manner.

As soon as Amadi left her, Aduke walked straight to her room and locked herself in. She took a long look at her shining engagement ring. It had come as a surprise, the greatest surprise of her life.

After Akin's disappointment she had begun to entertain serious doubts about her chances of ever getting married. She had been very fond of Akin and she knew he had loved her intensely. They had known each other for some time and had secretly resolved to marry before their parents knew anything about their friendship, although from the way his parents received her on the two occasions she visited them in his company, she was sure they admired her and liked her as a prospective daughter-in-law. Yet in spite of it all he had written her off. From the tone of his letter she knew he had acted under duress.

Aduke, he had written, *you know as well as I do how much I love you. I could not wish for a better girl as my wife. My parents also have nothing against you as a person. The only fly in the ointment is that unfortunate aspect of your family which I have already referred to. As soon as members of my family made the discovery they insisted that I must break things off unless I wanted them to cancel the plans for my University education.*

Aduke felt that, if Akin could use that excuse to wriggle away from her, any other Yoruba man would do the same. She could not believe she could love another boy as much as she loved him. His parents were well educated, his father was a graduate of Fourah Bay College and his mother a trained midwife. If their education could not prevent them from taking such a decision, what could she expect from illiterate prospective parents-in-law? That was why she had made up her mind not to think about marriage, to discourage any prospective husband, for fear of a last minute retreat on the man's part when his family discovered what Akin's family had discovered.

The idea of an Ibo husband had never crossed her mind before the Sweetie episode at the University. To her, the Eastern Region was as remote as Funtua; the possibility of ever settling there was even more remote. The Sweetie story suddenly revealed to her certain possibilities that had not occurred to her before. Amadi's tribal customs might be different from hers. What, to the Yoruba, might be a loathsome toad might be considered a choice dish among the Ibo. Amadi's decision to marry Sweetie was evidence too that tribal differences were not an insuperable obstacle.

As she sat in her room admiring her engagement ring, she wondered whether she should not disclose everything to Amadi. That was the least she could do as a Christian, the least she could do as a genuine friend, to make every fact available to him. After all, had she not accused him during the Sweetie episode of not placing all his cards on the table? The wisest thing was to call him in and tell him everything, even at the risk of losing the shining three-stone engagement ring.

But a voice told her she would be a fool to do such a thing. She was entitled to some happiness. Why should she throw away a golden opportunity for such a flimsy excuse? Why should she suffer through no fault of her own? There was nothing dishonest about her keeping silent over the issue. The onus lay on Amadi to find out what he liked about her family, in the same way as it was her responsibility to collect as much essential information as possible about Amadi. Amadi had told her nothing about his own family, why should she spread hers out like a mat before him? She was not anxious to find out anything about him. He had proposed to her out of his feeling for her and without any other considerations. She had accepted him without any strings, because of her affection for him. She thought people ought to marry that way. There was a growing tendency among young men and women to be too calculating, to check every detail, with the result that the people they married were often not the people they loved, but the people whose circumstances and family background fitted into a predetermined pattern.

23

Two days later Amadi found himself at the front of a lorry bound for Ilesha, Aduke's hometown. Events had moved fast, so fast that he was beginning to wonder whether he was rushing where angels would walk warily. He summed up the situation. Because of his entanglement with Sweetie, his parents had given him up; for about six months he had not heard a word from them, neither had he written to them. Because of Sweetie, his career at the University had had a white spot: he had been rusticated. He had been compelled to sign an undertaking to marry her for fear of being charged in court. At the very moment when he went to claim his child and seal the marriage pact his acquittal came, as unexpectedly as a torrential downpour on a dry harmattan afternoon.

A normal man in such circumstances would celebrate his freedom, rush back to the University, flash Sweetie's letter to his student friends and critics and ask the University authorities to expunge any reference to his rustication from the University records. He would allow himself some breathing space, some time to feel free before tying himself again to another woman. He would make peace with his parents, spring a pleasant surprise on them and teach them that it pays to trust your children. And if he wanted to be mischievous, to repay Chima in his own coin, he would travel to Ezinkwo to revive his attachment to Nwakaego. As a son of the soil he had a big advantage over Chima; the long association with Nwakaego's family, the early betrothal and the indebtedness of Nwakaego's family to his, were additional knock-out points.

Amadi did none of these things. Instead, he spent the money he had brought to Lagos for buying presents for his wife and child on an engagement ring for Aduke. The decision was instinctive; he had consulted nobody, not even himself. Back at the campus, he had not wasted more than twenty-four hours before slipping the ring on to Aduke's finger. Two days later he was on his way to Ilesha. To do what?

As he sat on the Ilesha-bound lorry he began to have second thoughts. What was he going to do at Ilesha? To bargain for a wife without consulting his parents, the same parents who had driven him away from home for falling into another woman's clutches? To bargain for a wife all by himself? What did he know of the Yorubas that he should fall into their hands single-handed? He knew very few Yoruba words beyond *ngbati* and *eku ise*. How could he be sure the Yorubas would not sell him with his eyes wide open? Had he, like a doomed dog, lost the sense of smell?

The lorry tore through space, disregarding the 35 miles per hour limit which the law imposed on lorries. Thick equatorial forest closed in on either side of the road and it was impossible to penetrate the vegetation even with the eyes. The forest extended for miles before the lorry emerged into a clearing. Here, the forest had been conquered by man; tree trunks scattered all over the place was evidence of this. A signboard indicated that the forest had been cleared for an experimental cocoa nursery by the Ministry of Agriculture.

The change in scenery had a salutary effect on Amadi's thoughts. His actions may have been impulsive, dictated by forces completely beyond his control, but now he began to feel that the forces would not lead him astray. Aduke was the central figure and she was such an adorable girl. Of the three girls with whom he had been closely associated, she was the only girl chosen entirely by himself. Nwakaego had been chosen for him before he knew the difference between a man and a woman; neither she nor Amadi had had a hand in the match. Their feelings had not mattered and the decision had been their parents' who felt they knew what was good for them. As for Sweetie, she had been chosen neither by his parents nor by him, but had captured him under false pretences.

Aduke was the girl he himself had won. Nobody had recommended her to him. He had taken the decision entirely by himself, and as the result of three years' personal observation. As intellectual equals with identical academic interests, they stood every chance of making excellent companions. The question of her tribe was insignificant. After all, had they not got on well as friends in spite of tribal differences? She would pick up the Ibo language very quickly. He could not go wrong by sticking to a girl like her.

It was she who had insisted on the trip to Ilesha. 'It is not,' she pointed out, 'our custom for a girl to accept an engagement ring from a boy without the consent of her people.'

'Come off it,' he had replied. 'How many of your customs do you still observe?'

'We may have dropped some of them, but our marriage traditions are still strong. I'll give you an example. A girl from my town was sent to England by her parents to learn how to become a secretary. On her arrival she had a happy reunion with her boy friend who had preceded her there. They got married before the year was out, a full-scale church wedding with invitation cards, wedding cake and everything. By the time they returned to Nigeria they had a bouncing son, and the girl was expecting her second child. Yet her parents, who had cabled congratulatory messages to the couple on their wedding day, refused to acknowledge that they were husband and wife until her husband and his relations had come to them to ask for her hand in the traditional manner. They also insisted on an engagement ceremony.'

Amadi knew she was right. 'What you say is true too of my people. I know of one case in which the couple got married in Germany and returned to Nigeria with three children. The girl's father locked up his daughter and her three children, and wouldn't release them until her husband had come to bargain for her hand as if she had never known a man!'

'If you knew that, why then do you object to our travelling to Ilesha to start off on the right foot?'

'I am only afraid of what the outcome may be. Suppose your family says no? Anything we did after that would be in deliberate disobedience to their wishes. On the other hand, if we just went ahead and announced our engagement it would be an accomplished fact, and we would merely ask for their blessing.'

'I think you are harbouring unnecessary fears.'

Ilesha was quite a large town. Like many Yoruba towns it was a mixture of modern well-built houses and rickety mud-walled single and double-storeyed houses. There was not a single house with a mat roof. All had roofs of corrugated iron sheets, some rusty with age, some shining offensively, some painted dark red.

'I wonder which is the house of Aduke's father? Would a girl born in a town this size, with so many shops, taxis, hospitals, secondary schools and modern houses, accept Ezinkwo as her home?'

The lorry stopped at the Ilesha motor park and Amadi stepped off. He did not look round for long before he saw Aduke waving to him; she came up leading a small child by the hand.

She looked him over admiringly. 'You look chic!'

'Thank you. I thought I should be decently dressed. First impressions count a lot, don't they?'

A taxi drove past. The driver gave them an enquiring glance, Aduke waved and in a trice he had stopped, reversed the car, pulled up beside them, thrown the front and rear doors open and shouted '*Nibo?*'

Aduke gave the address and they were off.

'Well, my dear, anything to report?' asked Amadi.

'Nothing in particular. I think I have practically won Mama over.'

'What about your father?'

Aduke appeared momentarily confused. 'I lost my father some years ago.'

'Oh, I'm very sorry. If I had known, I wouldn't have asked such a silly question.'

'My senior uncle will deputise for my father.'

'That's perfectly all right by me.'

The house to which Aduke took him was a modest double-storeyed house. It had originally had mud walls, but the mud had been replaced with burnt bricks. Amadi learned later that this practice was common in many Yoruba towns. A man with humble means puts up a simple mud-walled house and covers the top with corrugated iron sheets. Later, when circumstances improve, the mud walls are replaced bit by bit, either with burnt bricks or with cement blocks.

The settlement pattern looked different to that of Ibo towns; the houses were very close together and seemed to have no compounds. At Ezinkwo it was usual for a man to own more than one house, and to surround his large compound with a rectangular wall. The farm land he owned around his compound, further separated him from the next-door compound. The result was that in spite of its small population Ezinkwo covered a very extensive area with compounds dotted all over the town.

Inside the house, Amadi was taken upstairs and given a chair. From the window he looked out at the town, and the extensive rows of houses. The advantages of the Ilesha pattern of settlement became very obvious to him. It would be much easier to supply a town like this with amenities such as electricity, piped water and telephones than it would be at Ezinkwo, where people lived so far apart. Then another thought struck him. Living so close together without an efficient system of refuse disposal was bound to result in slums. He had not seen any 'little house' around and hardly any grass lawns where people could urinate. Was that why he had heard that the Yoruba towns were filthy? With people living so close together, infectious diseases would spread more easily than at Ezinkwo.

'*Epele, O Kabo.*'

Amadi turned sharply towards the door. A woman was greeting him. He stood up and bowed a good morning.

'*Se alafia ni?*' she continued.

'How are you?' Amadi asked, feeling embarrassed that he did not know the appropriate reply in Yoruba. He was relieved when Aduke walked in and explained to the woman that he did not understand Yoruba.

' She is my aunt.'

' I see. Please tell me, how should I greet her? '

' *Eku sinmi, Ma*, meaning, " Greeting on a Sunday or a holiday". When she asked you " *se alafia ni ?* " she meant " How are you? ". You should have replied " *Adupe, Ma* ".'

' *Eku sinmi, Ma. Adupe Ma. Eku sinmi, Ma. Adupe Ma.*' Amadi repeated the greetings, to get used to them.

' That's perfect. You're not doing badly.'

' I hope you'll teach me to speak Yoruba fluently. I shall feel lost otherwise.'

' There's plenty of time for that. Ha! ' she exclaimed, ' here comes Uncle. I don't want him to find us together.'

Amadi grew nervous. ' You're not going to leave me alone, Aduke? You know I don't know your language and you could see what a poor figure I cut with your aunt.'

' Don't worry, Uncle speaks some English, although I can't vouch that he remembers half the rules in Oliphant's English Grammar Book! ' And with that she skipped off.

Amadi licked his lips, pulled up his trousers, touched the knot of his University tie and looked himself over. He heard footsteps on the staircase, picked up a book he found lying on the window sill, sat down quickly and opening the book, pretended to concentrate. When, after a few seconds, he succeeded in focusing his eyes on the print, he discovered the book was written in Yoruba. It was too late to look for another one, so he stuck to it. His heart beat louder as the footsteps drew nearer.

The door opened. He shut the book and looked towards the door. A tall elderly man in woven *danshiki* walked in. Amadi got up and stood to attention.

' *Kabo*.' Aduke's uncle, Mr Olowu, greeted him first.

' *Adupe*, Sir,' Amadi replied, bowing low.

Mr Olowu said nothing. Amadi wondered whether he had said the wrong thing. Then he remembered which greeting came first.

' I am sorry, Sir,' he apologised, again with a low bow, hands behind him. ' *Eku sinmi*, Sir.'

'*Se alafia ni ?*'

'*Adupe*, Sir.' Amadi was pleased he had now got the order right.

'*Kabo* . . .' When Mr Olowu continued in Yoruba, Amadi looked sheepish. He knew he could not go on answering 'Yes, Sir' or he might answer 'yes' to a question requiring a negative answer. Neither could he stick to the non-committal 'Hm!' as he might reply 'Hm!' when something more detailed was required of him.

'I am sorry, Sir. *Mi ogbo*, Sir. In fact, I have been studying this book since I came, Sir, because I am anxious to learn Yoruba quickly, Sir.' He used 'Sir' liberally because he had been told that nothing pleased a Yoruba man more than to be so addressed.

Mr Olowu gnashed his teeth, pulled off his cap and placed it on a table near him. He was sitting on a stretcher kept at one corner of the sitting room. Amadi was still standing, waiting to be asked to sit. Mr Olowu seemed to be debating within himself whether or not he should speak in English. After a pause lasting about two minutes, he did so.

'Sit down.'

Another pause followed, broken by the entry of Aduke's mother. Amadi again stood up and repeated the greetings he had memorised. Aduke's mother smiled to hear him speak Yoruba. Although he did not understand the rest of what she said, he imagined she prayed for God's blessing on their marriage. He had been told that Yoruba prayers often ended with *Jesu Kristi Oluwa wa*.

Aduke's mother did not stay long. Silence followed her departure. Amadi suspected that Mr Olowu was looking him over; he was not sure whether he was pleased or displeased with what he saw. Emboldened by Aduke's mother's attitude and prayers, he decided to break the silence.

He stood up. 'Sir,' he addressed Mr Olowu, 'I think you know why I have come. I have been in the same class with Aduke in the University for three years, Sir. I like her very much, Sir. We believe we can become husband and wife, Sir, even though I am Ibo and she is Yoruba. So I have come to ask your permission, Sir, to marry her, Sir.'

Mr Olowu was again gnashing his teeth, and at the same time tapping one foot on the floor. He looked steadfastly in Amadi's direction. Amadi, who did not have the courage to look at him, stared at the floor waiting for the verdict.

'How you salute old people for your place?' he asked. Amadi could see he spoke with considerable effort at self-control.

'Sorry, Sir, I didn't hear what you asked, Sir.'

'I say, how you salute old people for your place?' This time it was impossible not to notice the anger in his voice. The purpose of the question baffled Amadi.

'We greet them " Good morning Sir ", or " Good afternoon Sir ". If they have titles we greet them by their titles, Sir.'

'Finish?'

'Yes, Sir,' replied Amadi, more confused than ever.

A silence followed. Amadi wiped the sweat off his brow and sat down.

'You say you want marry our daughter and you come ask my permission?'

'Yes, Sir,' answered Amadi, getting up from his chair.

Mr Olowu exposed his teeth in the driest of dry smiles. 'That na how people marry for your place?' he asked.

Amadi did not know every detail of the marriage customs at Ezinkwo. But whatever the customs might be, he knew it would be folly to answer 'no' to the question he had been asked. An affirmative answer would, if nothing else, show that whatever he did at Ilesha would have been acceptable in his own home town.

'Yes, Sir.'

'We no marry so,' observed Mr Olowu.

'May I know where I have gone wrong?' Amadi knew it was all over, and he no longer cared what he said.

'Me teach you how to marry our daughter?' Mr Olowu laughed at the big joke. '*Olorun gba mi O!*'

'I am sorry, Sir, if I have offended you. I do not know your custom.'

'If me be you, I for ask the custom first.'

In the silence that followed, Amadi sat down again.

Shortly afterwards the little girl who had accompanied Aduke to the motor park, came into the room, spoke to her uncle in Yoruba, took a long and curious look at Amadi and ran off. Mr Olowu followed her without saying another word to Amadi.

Amadi heaved a sigh of relief as Aduke walked in carrying a tray on which there was a covered dish, some cutlery and a tumbler. The little girl followed behind carrying a bottle of water.

'Well, how did it go?' asked Aduke.

'No luck at all. I think we ought to have planned the trip more carefully.'

'Did he refuse?' Amadi could read the anxiety in her question.

'We didn't get as far as that.'

Aduke laid the tray on a nearby coffee stool, placed the stool in front of Amadi, took the bottle from her little sister and poured out a glass of water.

'Here's something to eat. Uncle can be sticky at times but I'll soon find out from my mother what he's up to. We have one consolation. Mama has taken to you, and who wouldn't take to a young handsome "Kobokobo" like you?' She smiled admiringly.

'Spare your flattery for a more suitable occasion,' replied Amadi, though pleased with the compliment.

'I hope you'll not judge my cooking from this,' Aduke remarked as she withdrew. 'It's not easy to cook with firewood. My eyes are almost red. We'll soon have to be getting back to the University, so eat this now.'

Amadi gave her a full smile as she walked off. She was a sweet girl. The cloth she tied exposed her legs to advantage; just the kind of legs he had longed for during his secondary school days when he had idealised on the wife he would marry. What struck him most was the way in which she had taken the best from her mother—a pretty face—and added to that a fair skin and a good height. The legs? He had not observed her mother's legs very closely.

He uncovered the dish. The jolloff rice looked attractive. The leg of a chicken stood out above the rice, evidently from a bigger breed of fowl than those usually served at the University. His saliva flowed freely as he dug the spoon into the rice—the first mouthful of food cooked by his wife-to-be.

24

Amadi left Aduke at Oliaku Hall and walked to his own Hall. He had been pleased to learn from her that he had not made a complete fool of himself at Ilesha. As a person, he had cut as good a figure as any parent could wish for in a son-in-law—that point had been considerably stressed by Aduke's mother. According to her, it was bad enough to marry a 'Kobokobo'; the crime became intolerable if the 'Kobokobo' was, in addition, a midget. Why should a girl travel so far only to pick a midget? Aduke's mother was also thrilled to hear Amadi's efforts to speak Yoruba. As she could not speak English, her only hope of understanding her son-in-law depended on how well he learnt the Yoruba language. She prevailed on Aduke to do all in her power to ensure that he learnt it quickly.

Aduke had told him how she had tried to allay all her mother's fears. What would happen if Amadi died prematurely? Would it be safe to leave her in the hands of his relations, in such a far off land? Her mother would want Amadi to sign a written guarantee that Aduke would not forget them after their marriage, especially after they had spent so much on her education and waited patiently for her to complete her University career.

And what did Mr Olowu, the uncle, think of Amadi? 'An impudent ass who thought too much of himself and showed no respect for his elders,' he was told.

'During the short discussion I had with him before we left Ilesha, I discovered that his pride was hurt,' explained

Aduke. 'It's our custom to prostrate before our elders. Naturally, he expected you to prostrate as soon as he entered the room.'

'Me lie on the floor?' shouted Amadi. 'In my Terylene suit?'

'There's nothing ridiculous about that. Even our Premier prostrates himself in front of his father or an *Oba*. As a girl, I am expected to go on my knees and I always do so before my mother.'

'At Ezinkwo we prostrate only to God. As a matter of fact we do not even go that far; we bow to Him or at the most kneel on a sheet of newspaper.'

'It took me some time to convince him that you were not disrespectful, and that it was simply not your custom to prostrate before anybody. He was prepared to make allowances for today, and I promised him that you would not repeat it on another occasion.'

'What?' exclaimed Amadi. 'You mean, next time I meet him I shall fall flat for him?'

'Well, if you want me I'm afraid there'll have to be some give and take. I can show you the most convenient way of prostrating without lying flat on the ground.'

Mr Olowu had also been amazed that Amadi had had the audacity to stand before him and ask for the hand of his niece. Since marriage is a contract between families, not between a boy and a girl, it was improper for Amadi to go in quest of a wife himself, unless his father was dead and he had no other relations. Mr Olowu expressed his willingness to consider the proposal, provided it was made in the proper manner by Amadi's father, either by his coming to Ilesha in person or by a letter delivered by his emissaries. He also asked Aduke to tell Amadi that he did not know of any place in Yorubaland where a man went to ask for a girl's hand without bringing some drinks.

'In spite of our miscalculations and inexperience, I wouldn't dismiss the trip as a hopeless failure,' Aduke summarised. 'One thing is certain, my people now know where my interest lies. It may be an uphill task, but I'm certain we shall get there in the end. I've practically won Mummy over, and through her I hope to win Uncle over too. One fear I have is that my many aunts and my other uncles may poison their minds, now that our backs are turned.'

'My own fear is more serious than that,' observed Amadi. 'When I stood in front of your uncle to proclaim my intention, I knew I was doing the wrong thing. But I decided to gamble because that appeared to be my only hope. You know I've been out of touch with my parents for over six months, ever since they wrote me off on account of Sweetie. How on earth am I going to win them round and persuade my father to write to your uncle the sort of letter he expects?'

'Well, Amadi, we each have our problems, and it's no good thinking they're negligible. We'll just have to try our best and leave the rest to God. We're not getting married tomorrow. I believe the problems will sort themselves out.'

It was a worn-out Amadi who stood at the Porter's counter in Hall to ask for his room key. The Porter handed him a letter from his pigeonhole and made a fruitless search on the keyboard.

'Ah! I remember now. You get visitor for your room, Sir, so de key dey for your door.'

Visitor! Amadi felt like dodging his room. He was in no mood to receive a visitor. He had spent a whole day in a most unacademic manner, and he needed an interval of full, undisturbed rest to prepare for the cheerless routine that as a finalist he must get into again.

'Who is the visitor?' he asked.

'I no know, Sir. Na morning Porter who hand over to me who tell me say visitor dey for your room.'

'So the visitor has been in my room all this time?'

'I tink so, Sir. Of course me I come work for four o'clock so I no know what time de visitor come.'

'Whoever the visitor is should visit himself! I have no time for such ill-timed visits.' He walked out of the Hall, towards the sports stadium. Then he had second thoughts. A visitor who had waited so long for him would not be put off by a further delay of a few hours. Even if he ran away from his room, the visitor would be there waiting for him, as the burnt-out morning ash in the kitchen waits for the bachelor without a house-boy. His pace slowed down and he finally stopped, weighed up the situation again and turned back to his Hall.

' Only debtors run away from their houses. I do not owe anybody anything. But who could this mysterious visitor be? Could it be Sweetie? I hope not! In any case what could she be doing in my room? She could not have recovered sufficiently from her recent delivery to be setting another trap for me. And even if she has, she would have to be more foolish than a sheep to think that I would fall into her clutches again.'

He dismissed the idea. Anyway Sweetie would be too ashamed of herself to show up on the University campus so soon. Who then could it be? It could not be the Hausa hawker who had promised to bring him a set of ivory beads and earrings, in exchange for his old tweed jacket and two pairs of trousers. The set was intended as a surprise present for Aduke. There would have been no need for the Hausa man to wait, since he came to the campus almost every day.

When he opened the door of his room a young man was sitting on the cushion chair which Amadi had bought while he was teaching at Uwhuvbe. The man was half asleep, half awake, evidently worn out. His cream nylon shirt was dirty, especially round the collar even though he had carefully tied a handkerchief round his neck to protect it.

The man stood up hurriedly and clumsily. Amadi looked at him curiously and said:

' My name is Mr Chukwuka. I've been out of town since morning, and I've just been told that you've been waiting for me. I'm not sure I've met you before; in case I have, please pardon my forgetfulness. I am damn tired!'

' My name is Samuel Ejimofor, Sir, a native of Ajango. I'm teaching in the school in your town.'

' I see. I'm pleased to meet you.' Amadi advanced towards him and offered him his hand.

' Please sit down. Are you just visiting?'

' No, Sir, I've come to see you with a message from home. Can I get some water anywhere to drink, Sir?'

'Oh, sure.' As Amadi went to the fridge on the ground floor of the Hall to collect a bottle of iced water he felt very nervous. He mixed some squash for his guest and collected a saucer of biscuits for him. The man did not speak until he had eaten all the biscuits and drunk two glasses of squash. Amadi waited as anxiously as a man waiting outside the maternity ward while his wife is in labour.

'Well, Sir, your father is sick, and I have been sent to tell you about it and to take you home.'

Three drops of hot urine trickled down Amadi's left leg. Never in his life had such a message been sent to him. He felt certain his father was dead, and tears immediately began to form in his eyes. He tried to speak but a lump in his throat made it impossible. He pulled himself up, blew his nose and wiped his eyes with a handkerchief.

'Mr Ejimofor, I'm not a child. I know my father is dead and there's no need to hide it from me.' His voice shook and the tears were now flowing freely.

'I am telling you the truth, sir. Your father is not dead; I saw him yesterday before I left Ezinkwo. If he was dead, I would not be the person to be sent to bring such news to you.'

The sincerity in his tone brought some hope to Amadi.

'What's wrong with him?' he asked. 'For how long has he been sick?'

'For about one month. Some people say it is tuberculosis, some say it is a witch gradually eating his heart. Your father thinks it is something different again, but I do not know what name he calls it. Can we get a lorry tonight? I promised them that we would get to Ezinkwo tomorrow evening at the latest.'

Amadi left a message at the Porter's lodge for his Hall Warden, telling him that he had been forced to leave suddenly for his home town to see his father, who was critically ill. He then dashed off to Oliaku Hall to tell Aduke the unexpected news, and to borrow a couple of pounds from her for the trip, to be repaid when he returned to the campus. He had spent everything he had on the engagement ring. Aduke was very sympathetic.

'Can't I come with you, my dear?' she pleaded. 'I might come in useful one way or the other. And it would give me a chance of knowing where my future home is.'

'Not at this stage. I'm not even sure I shall find the old man alive. I've a feeling that he's dead and they don't want me to know the truth till I reach home.'

'Don't say that, Amadi. He can't be dead. You are letting your imagination carry you away.'

'Aduke, I can only pray that you are right. I just can't think of losing my father, and certainly not at this time when I am estranged from him. Oh no!'

'You'll find him alive, I'm sure. And make sure he is in the hands of a competent doctor before you leave home. I'll think of you and pray for you, and I'm sure everything will work out well. Give my love to my prospective parents-in-law, and God-speed.'

Amadi noticed an unsteadiness in her hand as she handed him five one pound notes, some of which she had borrowed from her neighbour without Amadi knowing.

When *No Telephone To Heaven* creaked to a halt by the Ezinkwo Postal Agency, Amadi stepped down with a heavy heart. There were some people in the market, but the market was not full. He did not bother to look for his mother, because he knew she would not be there. Mazi Nathaniel Ikwuaju was sitting alone by the Postal Agency; there were no palm wine drinkers. Amadi picked up his suitcase, tried to dodge Mazi Nati but greeted him when he saw he had been observed. The man's presence was an unfortunate coincidence. Amadi had enough to weigh him down without adding Nwakaego to it.

'I am happy you were able to return,' began Mazi Nati. 'I have been here since the market hour and I was beginning to wonder whether you would arrive today. Teacher, you have done very well. If you had not been around, who would have gone on such an errand for us?'

Amadi concluded that Mazi Nati had been sent to wait for him, no doubt to break the sad news to him in the customary tactful manner known to all elderly Ezinkwo men. He gave up all hope.

' Has he been buried? ' he stammered.

' God forbid! Do you bury a living person? Your father is still strong. We sent for you because you will know better than us how to find a good doctor to treat him. He told us that you warned him not to take any more injections from our people.'

The barometer rose. As they walked towards Amadi's father's compound Amadi, still in doubt, strained his ears women wailing or the singing of church hymns for the dead. All was quiet.

Some of the old men were sitting in his father's *obi*, but the usual warm welcome was not forthcoming, one or two merely lifted their hands in salutation. He walked quickly past them into the kitchen. His little brothers and sisters were sitting close together, a basket of boiled yams in front of them which they seemed to eat with little relish.

' Where is Mama? ' he asked them.

' In the room where Papa is,' they replied in unison, looking at him helplessly, yet hopefully. He was the person everybody was waiting for.

He dropped his suitcase and rushed into his father's room. His mother was sitting by the bamboo bed, tending the fire that warmed her husband.

' Papa! ' he shouted, tears streaming from his eyes. His mother stood up and embraced him. She, too, was crying. ' My dear son, you cannot imagine my joy to see you back. Satan has thrown a big temptation on us but, by the power of the Almighty God above, we shall conquer Satan. In the name of Jesus, we shall conquer.'

When she released him, Amadi bent down to touch his sick father. His eyes were open. He was still alive. He stared at his son for a while as if he could not recognise him.

' Papa! It's me. It's Amadi.'

His mouth slowly opened. ' Amadi – when – did – you return? ' He spoke in spasms.

' Just now, sir.'

' Who – asked – you – to – return? ' he continued.

Amadi's mother replied. 'Do you forget so quickly? Don't you remember you asked the teacher to go to the University to bring him back?'

'Oh – it is true –' The cough that followed frightened Amadi. It lasted for a full minute, and each time he coughed Amadi thought he would cough out his heart. When it ended he spat a thick misture of sputum and blood into a pot of sand held up to him by Amadi's mother.

'He has been coughing like this for more than four native weeks,' she explained.

He closed his eyes and breathed rapidly for a while. When his breathing returned to normal, he opened his eyes again and looked at Amadi.

'Amadi!' he called.

'Sir?'

'How – is – your – wife?' At this question his face became tense and his eyes more prominent.

'I am not married, sir, I did not marry that girl. It turned out that the child she was expecting was not my own, but belonged to one white man. As a result I did not marry her.'

The tense face relaxed, giving way to a smile of relief. For the first time since his return, Amadi had some hope that the muddy water would soon clear.

'Amadi – Missus –' Son and mother looked at the sick man in expectation.

'If I die now – I shall be – happy.'

'You have started talking nonsense again,' interrupted Amadi's mother. 'I have told you, you will not die. We have not stolen anybody's goat. We have not killed anybody. This temptation will go back the way it came.'

The sick man went on speaking, each word dragged painfully out between long pauses.

'Amadi – I am – glad. I knew – you did not – do it. My own son could not – do such a thing. Nwakaego – would have been engaged to the D.O. But – I told her father to wait – for you. Oh! I have talked – too – much. But promise me – that you will – marry Nwakaego and I shall – give you all my last blessing and – die – a happy – man.'

'Papa! what are you saying?'

'Have – you – promised?'

His mother looked at him pleadingly. 'My son, please promise him. Do anything that will save his life.'

'Yes, sir. I promise.'

Again the words came slowly and painfully, with long rests between each word.

'I am now happy. Very happy. Mazi Nati will now – forgive me. If – I – die now, I shall lie quiet – in my grave – and not worry to find out – whether you have married a foreigner – or a prostitute. Give me – your – hand. Your mother knows I am not owing – anybody – anything. She knows all – my property, all – my land. God will bless you – and – Nwakaego and give you many – children. You will –'

He stopped suddenly. His eyes bulged. A violent cough seized him. He was in agony, his legs and arms threshed the bed in convulsive jerks.

'Papa!' shouted Amadi, holding him as if trying to rescue him from unseen powers. His mother rushed out to the men sitting in the *obi* to ask them to come and help. The struggle was still going on when they came in. They held him firmly by the arms and legs. He coughed violently again, passed some slimy excrement and urine, groaned loudly and became limp.

25

Amadi returned to the campus a confused man. This time the long miles between Ezinkwo and the University appeared too short. Never had he felt so incapable of giving direction to his thoughts. He badly needed someone to whom he could unburden his heart before it exploded.

This was the first death in his family, his first direct

encounter with death. He had always shown concern for bereaved families, sometimes to the point of shedding a few tears in private. But such concern was the concern felt by an outsider. As they said at Ezinkwo, a corpse on its way to the grave could be no more than a bundle of firewood to a passer-by. It was a very different matter when the corpse belonged to a member of your family, to your father. Mazi Onuzulike Chukwuka had been a worthy father, a shining example to his children and to the small Christian community at Ezinkwo.

'It's that boy who broke his heart and killed him. Whoever heard of "the man who planted more yams than guinea fowls could eat" being sickly?' The discussion had ended abruptly as Amadi was seen, but he had heard enough to add to his sorrow.

'Could it be that I am responsible for Papa's death?' He tried many times to dismiss the unwholesome thought but it lingered on.

'I don't see any link between marrying Sweetie and developing a serious cough. In any case, I made it clear that the Sweetie affair was a thing of the past, and I promised to marry Nwakaego, his choice for me. That should have saved him, if his sickness had been caused by my connection with Sweetie.'

'Imagine suffering so much for your child', people had said, 'and not living to drink his water even for one day! Nothing could be worse, especially when the time for eating and drinking was so imminent.'

Amadi saw all the plans he had made for his father buried with the wooden coffin that carried his corpse. He knew very well all the privations his father had suffered, all the sacrifices he had made to give his son a good education. He knew that it was for his welfare, and the welfare of his brothers and sisters, that the 'husband of yams' toiled relentlessly the best part of each day. He had looked forward to the day he would compel his father to take life easy and to enjoy himself. He had made up his mind about the regular monthly allowance he would send to each of his parents as soon as he began to work. He would invite each of them to his house to spend weeks, resting and eating. Perhaps one day he would be able to buy a small secondhand car for them . . .

The two weeks he spent at Ezinkwo before returning to the campus were the most trying he had ever spent in his life. The sight of his father putting up a last struggle for life returned to him frequently, like an unwanted reflection in a mirror. The tears he shed the day his father had died would have been enough to wash away the thick coat of dust on his mother's clothes as she flung herself again and again to the ground, moaning for the husband who was oblivious of her grief.

Gradually he had learnt to keep back his tears. He had to.

' My son, you cannot continue weeping like a woman. You are now a man; your grief should be channelled to your heart, not to your eyes.'

' My man, you cannot accompany every sympathiser who bursts into tears. Leave that to your mother and your sisters. If you weep like that, who will console the women? '

' My son, I hope you are taking note of all the people who have brought cloth to cover your father's body. It is very important that you do so.'

' Amadi, my son, I hear you will be returning to your University very soon. It is good. I just want you to know that your father has no enemies at Ezinkwo so you need not fear for the safety of his property. We shall help your mother with the farm work, but you must ask her not to try to work like the " husband of yams ".'

Amadi had been mentally unprepared for his sudden metamorphosis from a carefree undergraduate to a father to his younger dependants, and a son-cum-husband to his mother. He had no choice. Before he left for the University he had made discreet enquiries about his father's land and other property, ensured that his younger brothers and sisters would continue at school, and that enough of his father's farm work would be continued to provide for his mother while he was still a student.

The parting from his mother was painfully brief.

' My son, God is wide awake. Nothing is beyond him.'

' Yes, Ma.'

'Make sure you do not forget us. Write frequently.'

'Yes, Ma.'

'Write to Nwakaego and tell her everything that has happened. She is my one consolation.'

'All right, Ma. You must promise me that you will stop crying. Papa is dead; he cannot return to earth even if we cry our eyeballs out.'

'Oh! My son.'

But as Amadi picked up his small suitcase to make his way to the Postal Agency, his mother's tear ducts appeared doubly activated. He bit his lips and walked off with his head held high in an effort to restrain his own tears.

Back at the campus, his first thought was to dodge Aduke. That would give him an opportunity to weigh all the issues before confronting her.

'But how can I dodge her? We are in the same class and attend the same lectures. She knows my room number and where to find me practically any hour of the day. I might more easily dodge my shadow!'

Write to her! The idea dropped from the ceiling and he was extremely grateful to whoever threw it down.

That's the only way out. Write to her. Tell her everything. That would save the discomfort of standing before her to render a most difficult account of his fateful trip home.

He searched his drawer for a writing pad. Immediately he had written 'My darling Aduke' his pen seemed to dry up. He discovered he did not know what to write, or what he meant by 'everything'.

'How can I tell her that the pendulum has swung over to Nwakaego? Was Nwakaego not the same girl I had sworn by my ancestors that I could never marry? How can I convince Aduke that I was not feeding her on lies when I told her I had written Nwakaego off? How can I convince her that I have not merely been making a fool of her, turning her into my football?

'Why, in any case, should I kick Aduke out? She is the girl of my choice. How can I dismiss her after buying her an engagement ring and travelling to Ilesha to announce to her people my intention to marry her? Is it fair to break my promise to her in order to carry out another promise?'

'Remember, young man, the promise to marry Nwakaego is now a promise to the dead!'

Amadi made as if he wanted to grab that inner voice and crush it to nothing. He ended up trying to argue with it.

'Yes, it may be a promise to the dead, but it was made at a time when I was mentally unbalanced. I was driven to it in an attempt to save Papa's life. Papa died in spite of the promise. Why then should I be bound by it? Is it fair that I should lose both ways?'

'All that logic will not help,' persisted the voice. 'A promise to the dead is a promise to the dead. You know what it means at Ezinkwo.'

Of course Amadi knew. He knew the popular belief that to break a promise to the dead was to invite trouble from the land of the spirits. But was this belief really true? Has it not also been said that dead men do not bite? Have not Israel Nwaoba and his Three Night Wizards stated in one of their well known songs that 'when a man is dead, he's gone forever'?

The voice reminded him of Agodi Onwuka who had broken the promise made to his late father. Where was he now? In the graveyard. Why? Because he thought he was wiser than his great-grandfathers. His dead father gave him a crack on the head beneath the apple tree and that was the end of Agodi Onwuka.

'What am I to do with Aduke?' Amadi asked helplessly.

'Tell her that you cannot marry her,' the voice replied.

Amadi covered his face with his hands. Then he suddenly jumped up and paced his room as he summarised the situation.

'Most unfortunate. Lose my father. Get involved with two girls with conflicting claims. My degree examination round the corner. Most unfortunate. Terribly unfair!'

The voice had dried up. After waiting in vain for it to speak, Amadi continued.

'I know what I'll do. I shall simply present the whole episode to Aduke, underlining the likely hazards on our way. Instead of telling her that I have decided this way or that,

I shall ask for her guidance. Let her suggest the wisest solution, the most appropriate way of "carrying this child with the fractured waist".'

He sat down, picked up his pen and continued from where he had left off. A knock on the door switched his thoughts. He turned towards the door, at the same time grunting a hostile ' Yes? ' The door opened and Aduke walked in.

Amadi's face passed through a series of rapid metamorphoses. The first was of a man angry at an intruder invading his thoughts; then the expression changed to that of a man receiving a surprise visit from a friend most welcome at any other time than the present; then the face of conscience: a stricken boy caught with his fingers deep in the soup pot; and finally to the face of the embarrassed man who realises that he is not being sufficiently nice and warm to his guest.

She deposited her bag with its flask and some fresh fruit on the writing table and came close to Amadi.

' I got your telegram some days ago.'

' He died the day I arrived home.'

Aduke threw her arms round him, then slumped down on her knees by the bed and buried her face in the sheet. Amadi was utterly helpless as he watched her sob. His father's death scene flashed back, with his widowed mother sobbing her heart out by the bed. Superimposed on this was the faint outline of the girl he had promised to marry, now inevitably drifting farther and farther away from him, as the minutes following his father's death lengthened into hours and days. A few heavy tears ran down his cheeks and finally found their way into his mouth. He wiped them away quickly and bit his lower lip in an effort to regain self-control. As the mist in his eyes cleared, he thought he saw Nwakaego smiling radiantly at him with both hands on her hips, as if she was saying: ' Now, Sir, are you coming back to me? ' She seemed to have developed full maturity overnight.

' Oh!' grunted Amadi, as if in protest. ' How can I survive all this! What am I to do? '

He lifted Aduke on to the bed and sat down beside her, utterly confused. For some time after she had stopped sobbing they sat in silence. When she rose to go he, too, rose automatically.

' I know it's difficult, but please try and be calm. I will do all I can to help.'

As she emptied the contents of her bag, Amadi noticed that she wore the engagement ring. She saw him staring at it.

' I put it on the day your telegram arrived. I hope it's all right to wear it? '

' Y-yes.'

26

After many unfinished attempts, Amadi put the final full stop to the letter late that night. He was satisfied that he had covered all the ground: the traditional opposition at Ezinkwo to the marriage of girls from distant towns, his long connection with Nwakaego, the Sweetie affair and the suggestion at Ezinkwo that his attachment to Sweetie had broken his father's heart and finally caused his death. Then he dealt with his profound love for Aduke, and how he had travelled home hoping to announce their engagement at the opportune moment, and to return to the University with the letter for Aduke's family. Then the fateful promise, made with the best of intentions to a dying man, but no less binding for that. Being a son of Ezinkwo, he knew the hazards that lay in wait for them if they pressed on with their plans and got married. He did not wish to add to these hazards the effect such a wedding might have on his mother. His love for Aduke, however, was so profound that he wanted to be guided by her advice. If she thought they should unite against the dead and the unpredictable forces of the spirit-world, he was willing to go along with her. If she thought they would be foolish to fight unseen powers, then . . .?

Before setting off for lectures the following morning, he

read through every word of the long letter and nodded his head with satisfaction. It could not have been better written. The significance of every word had been well considered. He sealed the envelope and handed it to the Hall messenger, with the instruction that he should deliver it to Oliaku Hall between eleven o'clock and midday.

Amadi had a restless afternoon. He knew Aduke must have read his letter and he kept imagining what her reaction would be.

At five o'clock he walked to the Porter's lodge at Niger Hall and picked up the telephone.

' Oliaku Hall, please.'

' Oliaku Hall Porter's Office here. Which person you want? '

' May I know whether Aduke is in? '

' Who? '

' I mean Miss Olowu.'

' You be student here or you be stranger? '

' I am a student,' replied Amadi, coldly. He decided this was not the time to quarrel with officious and illiterate Hall Porters.

' Abi you never hear wetin happen to Miss Olowu? '

' What are you talking about? Are you sure you know the person I am talking about? '

' Me know Miss Olowu? Me wey don' work for Oliaku Hall so-tee! Miss Olowu no be de gal dem carry jus' now go Abeokuta Mental Hospital? '

' What! ' Amadi could hardly hold the receiver. Every part of his body trembled. The Niger Hall Porter beside him, suspended his work, infected by Amadi's anxiety.

' Ah! I hear say 'e get one letter so from 'im boy friend— dat "Kobokobo" boy dem call Mr Chukwuka. Me I no know wetin 'e write for dis letter. After Miss Olowu read am 'e begin do as if 'e mad. Dem don carry am go Abeokuta Mental Hospital. Some people wey know-am proper for Ilesha say na de same ting wey kill 'im Papa. Dem say 'e run mad one afternoon, kill one of 'im own pikin with matchet and run inside bush . . .'

The receiver dropped from Amadi's hand. He could hear no more. His head swirled like a dust storm at Nsukka. Everything went blank. He drifted towards his room like a sleepwalker, like a priest in a trance. Instinctively he inserted the key into the keyhole, opened the door and stumbled into his room.

In front of the wardrobe stood his father, in the white robe in which he had been buried a fortnight ago. He had a half-smile on his lips, like a father looking down on a stubborn child who, neglecting every entreaty, plunges a piece of red pepper into his mouth, to judge for himself how it tastes.

Amadi shrieked violently at the sight, shut his eyes tight with his two palms and collapsed on to the bed.

THE END

Notes

Some notes from the author on Ibo and Yoruba words and the
origins of some Ibo sayings. Ibo is the language of the Ibo people
who live in Eastern Nigeria and Yoruba that of the Yoruba in
Western Nigeria.

The notes are under the number of the chapter to which they
refer and where a word is not described as Yoruba it belongs to
the Ibo language.

1

Akwasa	Ibo exclamation, normally indicating admiration of an object or person. In common use among teenagers.
King Jaja of Opobo	King Jaja reigned in Opobo, a town in the Rivers Province of Nigeria, during the nineteenth century.

3

Oyibo	European, or pertaining to a white person. Means here the English language.
Supu	Ibo slang, normally used to indicate that a speaker is making use of high-sounding words.
Akwukwo	Book. Used here to symbolise a learned person.

4

Agbada	Voluminous gown worn by men.
Rapukwam na twelve akugo	The literal translation is: 'Leave me, for it is now twelve o'clock'. A girl is pleading with her boy friend to let her go as her parents would be cross with her if she came home after midnight.

Aka mere	Hand-made. This expression is used to differentiate between locally distilled gin, which the people distill with their own hands, and imported gin.
Nzogbu! *Enyi mba enyi!*	A song, symbolising the crushing effect of an elephant on its prey or enemy.

5

Ewo!	Exclamation, similar to 'Oh!'
Onye bulu	Porters. They usually carry their load on their heads.
Anata	'Has returned'. Ibo children often chant *Papa anata, Oyo-yo! Mama anata, Oyo-yo* when their father or mother comes home from the farm, market, or any distant journey.
Afe itepu	Blouse.
Pili pili	Watery.
Agidi	Soft meal prepared from corn flour.
Otu Onicha	The popular name for a large market at Onitsha, a town on the River Niger.
Akwu acha	A yam disease which turns the leaves of yam tendrils from green to yellow.
Chi	Personal God as distinct from the God of the community. Sometimes used to refer to Fate.
Obasi-on-high	The Supreme God.

6

Obi	House for the head of the family, this is where he usually receives his guests.

7

Ike Kute	A name indicating that only the physically strong could fetch water from the stream.

8

Jioji	Cotton, or sometimes silk, material, often patterned with brightly coloured checks.

Abacha ncha	Meal prepared from boiled and dried slices of cassava.

9

Ikeji	Festival to mark the yam harvest.
Mgbedike	A mask with a large head, usually dreaded because of the large sharp matchet it carries and which is kept under control by means of a strong rope tied round the mask's waist.
Odo	Another type of mask, dirty brown in colour.
Nna anyi	Literally means 'our father'. An elderly man was often called *Nna anyi* by younger people including his wife and children, as a mark of respect.
Udu	A musical instrument. A pot with a long neck and a small round hole on one side.
Shekere	A musical instrument. A calabash with a network of small black seeds on the outside.
Abacha ncha	See above.
Cassava foo foo	Boiled and pounded cassava, usually a heavy meal.
Agbada	See above.

10

Ama kekwu	*Ama kekwu* literally means 'No matter what people say'. The dance is appropriately youthful and carefree.
Ndo	Expression of sympathy or sorrow, similar to 'Sorry!'; 'What a pity!'; 'How sad!'

12

Oliaku	Literally: 'Consumer of wealth'. It is used as a greeting for married women.
Iroko	A huge tree: very tall and with a very massive trunk which yields strong timber. It is virtually impossible to climb the iroko tree when it is full grown.
Olorun ma je	Yoruba for 'God forbid'.

Odi egwu	Ibo expression similar to 'Wonderful!'; 'Amazing!'; 'Terrific!'.

Olorun gbami O	Yoruba for 'God save me'.

The Nsugbe coconut	The Ibos have a roundabout procedure for breaking bad news, to minimise the shock to the recipient. To ignore this customary procedure, or to speak openly on something regarded a secret, is to break the Nsugbe coconut.
Obodo oyibo	Literally means 'white man's town', but is used primarily to refer to the United Kingdom.

Mba mmiri	Ibo for a riverine town.
The town crier's 'ogene'	'Ogene' is a hollow metal, open at one end; more commonly used as a musical instrument, but it is also used by the town crier when he makes his rounds to proclaim an important announcement.

Makakwu	Slang for 'nit-wit'.

Rora O	Yoruba for 'take it easy'.

Ngbati	Yoruba for 'when'.
Eku ise	Yoruba greeting for somebody at work.
Nibo?	Yoruba, short for 'where are you going?'
Epele O, Kabo	Yoruba for 'How do you do? Welcome'.
Se ala fia ni	Yoruba for 'How do you do?' 'How are you?'
Eku simi	Yoruba greeting for someone who is resting. It is used on Sundays as well as holidays.
Adupe	Yoruba for 'Thank you'.
Danshiki	A sleeveless jumper.
Kabo	Yoruba for 'Welcome'.
Mi ogbo	Yoruba for 'I don't hear'; 'I don't understand'.
Jesu Kristi Oluwa wa	Yoruba for 'Jesus Christ Our Lord'.
Olorun gba mi O	Yoruba for 'God save me, Oh!'

Oba	Yoruba for 'Chief' or 'King'.